CRAZY MOON ZOO

Withdrawn

CRAZY MOON ZOO

a novel by **DAN POTTER**

franklin watts • new york • london
toronto • sydney • 1985

Library of Congress Cataloging in Publication Data

Potter, Dan.
Crazy moon zoo.

Summary: Seventeen-year-old Jory struggles to
deal with his anger, confusion, and resentment
of his older brother as he seeks to discover
how he fits into the universe.
[1. Self-acceptance—Fiction.   2. Emotional
problems—Fiction.   3. Brothers—Fiction]   I. Title.
PZ7.P8517Cr   1985   [Fic]   85-6157
ISBN 0-531-10076-6

c . 1

CRAZY MOON ZOO

PART ONE

THE BOY

I'm up in my room, practicing. Practicing for life, I think. In front of the mirror, I strike poses. Thumbs in my belt, I'm a race car driver; I've just won the Grand Prix.

Hands on hips I'm the star of the Super Bowl: I kicked a seventy-five-yard field goal. A hundred thousand fans go wild.

Nothin' to it, I tell the press. *Clean livin'. Lots of Wheaties . . .*

I glide toward the mirror, practicing my cat walk.

Clint the Cat's back in town, somebody whispers.

Cool as snow I ease into a room . . .

Hey, Clint, a guy says. *Where'd you get that girl you were with last night?*

Wiggled my little finger, I say.

For a minute there's this guy in the mirror I hardly know. Jory Hall, seventeen; 2120 Filmore Street. His eyes are full of question marks. His whole posture's a stifled exclamation mark. I turn away; the game's more fun.

From the closet I grab a raincoat and a beat-up hat. I pull the brim down low over my face. I slip the gun from beneath my mattress.

It's not loaded and it's one of my secrets. I found it in an alley and nobody knows about it but my friend, Bud. Now I shove it inside my right coat pocket.

OK, I say, to the baddest guy in the world: *When I say move,* jump! *When I say stand still,* freeze!

I put the gun back in hiding. A guy needs a few secrets, I think. But I've got one or two I could do without.

Anyway, I like the image in the coat. I've got a good sneer. The trouble is, it's too hot outside for a raincoat. Besides, the rain's stopped and there's no one there to sneer at except the guy I hardly know . . .

2

Saturday night I'm telling Bud: "I'll get a super job this summer. I'll buy a Trans Am. A blue job with a white racing stripe. It's gotta have white leather seats and quadraphonic sound. And I'll—"

"What're we gonna do *tonight?*" Bud says.

"I don't know," I tell Bud. "I'll think of something."

We're matching pennies on the way downtown. Now that the rain's stopped, the streets gleam like quarters. I know some guys who're so crazy they'd match streets.

A car's zooming up Maple Street and I step off the curb and raise my arm for it to halt. It's a Porsche. *Achtung!* Tires screech like witches and this guy sounds off out the window.

"Watch where you're goin', kid!"

"Pedestrians first," I say.

"Wise kid."

"You got it."

The trouble with adults, I think, is that they've lost their sense of humor. *Then why don't you laugh more?* a little voice says.

"Come on," I tell Bud. "Race you to Pete's."

3

I guess I think I can outrun it, whatever it is. There's this thing, see, in the back of my mind. It's like a picture you can barely see. Just when I'm about to focus on it, it fades out.

Main Street's a contest of neon and cars. Pedestrians lose. In a shoving match, Bud and I make it to Pete's Poolarama out of breath. The whole place is cigar-colored and the smoke's thick enough to slice. Another teenage paradise.

I enter like I'm wearing the raincoat with my hat pulled down. Two guys wave, and I give a short wave back from the hip.

From the wall I grab a cue stick and tell Bud to rack 'em. Bud gets about three shots in and I run the table. This older dude challenges me and I beat him, too. He hands me fifty cents.

"Give me a chance to win my money back," he says.

"Sure. On your fifty-fifth birthday."

He glares and I walk out like Clint the Cat. Bud follows; Bud likes to be led. Outside, neon signs flash weak come-ons. The thing is, stores have everything but what you really need.

We're hanging loose on the street and Bud's waiting for me to come up with an idea. But all of a sudden I'm teed off. Maybe because Dad wouldn't let me have the car . . .

No . . . Something else: it flashes like a picture; then it's gone. I kick over a litter basket and we start running. We head for the park.

I'm not, nor have I ever been, a *real* Crazy—except for one night in August under a full moon that looked like an emergency room for the whole Earth. A real Crazy is someone—anyone—who really has to get out of It before they're sure what It is.

I was a part-time Crazy. I was only half out of It; I half knew what It was.

The real Crazies in high school were guys—or girls— who were self-conscious, didn't feel so hot sometime, and didn't like where they were. So they drank—or smoked or pilled or popped—a lot and got paranoid, threw up, and didn't *know* where they were.

The real Crazies also jumped out of windows, had car wrecks, freaked out in public places, and got sent to asylums.

I was scared of drugs. Maybe that's why I was a part-time Crazy. My solution was to keep on the move a lot. "Americans love to move," one of my teachers said. He mentioned a man who moved so much he forgot where he lived.

Bud and I were always racing something: neighborhood dogs, flashy cars, each other. As we bounded down the street that night, I didn't know it, but before the summer was over, I would outrun myself . . .

4

Away from cars and neon signs, I'm almost sane on the park bench. Sometimes I think man's best friend is not a dog—it's a tree. But it's funny: I don't want Bud to know I like trees and stuff. He thinks I'm a man of action.

"I'm waitin'," Bud says.

"And I'm thinkin'. I'm thinkin'."

It's early spring and a full moon plays hide and seek with ragged clouds. I watch swans glide on the mirror-still water. *Can swans ice-skate?*

A couple ambles past—citizens from another planet. People in love walk like Siamese twins. They have their own language. And they make me want to twitch.

I'm wiggling my knees like a daddy long legs in a corner. It's like all those times with a battle inside and nothing to fight it with. Bud pulls out a cigarette and I frown.

"Why do you smoke those things? You'll pollute the swans."

"Nothin' better to do."

I have no answer for his answer, so I watch the swans. Nothing seems to bother them; nothing at all.

I've got this reputation for coming up with crazy ideas. I guess it started after we put the Dorns' pet goat in the music room at school. It didn't do much but mess up the floor and eat the teacher's orange beret. But the thing is, once you start with crazy ideas, you can't stop—they have to get crazier.

Tonight I'm a blank. And Bud's going on and on about taking groceries to some old lady.

". . . I unloaded the box in the kitchen, and Miss Elkins was in the living room with a neighbor. She said she always left her keys in the car at night. Said she read somewhere that car thieves don't give up when they don't find the keys. They just go in the house and get them. Miss Elkins said she'd rather have them take the car that's insured than come in the house and bother her . . . Man, those old ladies are really somethin'."

Bud's getting nervous again and I say it because I've got nothing else to say.

"How'd you like to go for a nice ride?"

"Where? *How?*"

"Don't you understand anything? That car's just sittin up there in the drive—with the keys in it."

"Aw, man," Bud says. "You wouldn't do *that*, would you?"

That's all it took.

"Come on," I say.

5

There's this feeling pushing me—adrenalin, I guess. I'm still kind of mad and I don't know what's bugging me. But halfway there I get to thinking it's not such a great idea. Besides, it's kid stuff. I slow down and Bud says:

"You gonna chicken out?"

"Are you kiddin'?"

So I'm not thinking at all. I just move.

We hide behind trees in Miss Elkins's yard. Upstairs in her bedroom she's watching TV: a bluish flicker lights one wall. The neighbors are either gone or hibernating behind drawn blinds. It's cloud-still. I wish I had my raincoat and the hat with the brim pulled down.

"She won't hear a thing," I say. "Just to be sure, we'll push it out in the street. Then we'll start it up and—*zoom!*"

"What if someone comes by?"

"Pessimist. Now who's chicken?"

The car door clicks open and moonlight flashes on the keys. I ease the car out of gear and we roll it out in the street. Just to be safe we push it another half block.

I'm driving and we make it the first few blocks without turning on the lights. I can't believe how easy it is.

And it's neat, tooling through the streets in a brand-new Buick.

"Where you wanta go?" Bud says.

"To the moon."

"Gas costs too much."

"We'll keep off the main streets. Let's head out on the old highway."

Ace driver Jory speeds through the south part of the city. The highway's a black invitation engraved with moonlight. I take it and get the car up to eighty.

Bud's conscience, the size of a barn, crowds him. He tells me to slow down and I tell him he worries too much.

He keeps glancing all around, like he's expecting a police car behind every billboard or rushing at us with whirling red lights from every side road.

"Come on, Jory. Let's take it back."

"We went to all the trouble to—borrow it. Let's have some fun."

Fun's one of my favorite words: it's a three-letter sound for half-crazy.

I don't want Bud to know I'm a little worried, too, so I get music on the radio and hum along with Debby Boone. Right away, I'm in a different mood.

Like a moon-eyed kid, I'm missing something I have no words for. Even the moon is different: a symbol for all those feelings I have; the ones I don't talk about . . .

I glance up to see this big white dog flash across the highway.

"Look out!" Bud yells.

The car swerves when I slam on the brakes. There's a *thump* and the dog disappears in a blur and we screech, swaying across the highway. I fight the steering wheel and we slide off the road and stop.

I can smell burning rubber when we get out. The dog's lying in the ditch all crumpled up.

"Dumb dog," I say.

"Aw, man. We killed it."

"It's just a dumb dog."

"But we *killed* it."

"Come on. Let's go."

I drive back like nothing's bothering me, but I'm thinking: *Another stupid mistake. That's all you do, Jory—goof up. High school's almost over and you haven't done anything but make mistakes. Not like Reve. Not like Reve at all . . .*

(My brother Reve graduated three years ahead of me, and Reve did it all: got the grades of a genius, played sports like a pro, and was the all time Romeo of Marshal High.)

"Hey, Jory," Bud says, punching my arm. "Where you goin', anyway?"

We've passed Miss Elkins's house. And I back up and pull into the drive. It was a good caper, I think. We pulled it off just right.

Then a black and white car pulls into the drive behind us and two cops jump out.

"Don't move," one of them says.

I'm not about to move; I can't. But Bud makes a run for it and gets halfway down the drive before he's caught. The other one holds my arm and guides me toward the back steps where Miss Elkins stands like a whooping crane.

"Are those hoodlums armed?" she asks.

"No. They're just kids."

Miss Elkins adjusts her glasses and cranes her long white neck.

"Well, Jory Hall. I can't believe my eyes."

By this time the other cop brings Bud up to where we're standing. Miss Elkins looks Bud over, too.

"And Bud Mavis. Whatever possessed you boys?"

"The full moon," I say.

6

What started out to be a lark is now a vulture.

On the way downtown, I'm wondering what you're supposed to do—offer a bribe? Then I think: Jory, you couldn't bribe your way out of a phone booth.

The police station is a small brick building the color of iodine on a gash of a street just off Main. Inside: about four shades of gray and three shades of brown—including the people. They look at Bud and me as though we've burned a flag.

I can't believe I'm actually going to end up in jail—not Jory the Great. But the door closes like a loud good-bye. They've got Bud down the corridor somewhere, and I'm glad: he can't see my green face.

Thinking of all the things I might have said, I pace the cage I'm in. The cage gets smaller and smaller. The worst is yet to come: I haven't faced my parents.

Over against one wall something moves. I've been so busy debating what I'll tell Dad, I haven't seen this old guy lying there on the steel bunk. He makes sounds like a rundown machine. He sits up.

"Dubney Perkins," he says, and a shaky hand paws the stale air.

His hand is like a warm washcloth, rough and wet, and his face is all pink and worn. It makes me think of a half grapefruit left in the air too long. I won't mention his clothes; his clothes were unmentionable.

"Dubney? Never heard that name before."

"Probably never will, either. You can call me Dub."

"I'm Jory."

"Well, out with it. What have you done? Confession's good for the soul."

He moves over a little and I sit beside him. He smells like the air does when you pass a bar—a seedy bar.

"We didn't do anything much—just took a car."

"*Just?* . . . You know why you did it?"

"Nothin' better to do. We were just—messin' around."

"Mankind gets in a lot of trouble," he says, "for this reason: doing something simply because there's not one good reason—at the moment—not to . . ."

He reminds me of a college professor or someone who taught high school before I was born. And despite the shape he's in, I get a nice feeling.

"Ever been arrested?" he asks.

"Yeah. A few times."

I get to making up this stuff about how I've been busted. I'm telling a long story about driving a Trans Am ninety miles an hour through the streets with the cops behind me. He's eyeing me funny, as though I've changed nationalities.

"How about you? Been busted before?"

"About a hundred times."

"You're kiddin'."

"I wish I were, my boy. I wish I were."

"How come so many times? You don't look like a criminal to me."

"I'm what is known as a public drunk. I got that unenviable reputation for one reason: I *am* a public drunk."

Dub helps keep my mind off the showdown: facing

my parents, especially Dad. But I can't look at him too long. His eyes pull you in—down—like sad quicksand.

"Tell me about yourself," he says.

"Not much to tell."

"Give me a few headlines."

So I rattle off a glorious fake story about what a great athlete I am. I'm telling him about all the girls that hang around, and all the time he's studying me like I'm a used book.

"What's the matter?" I say.

"I've got you pegged for a loner."

"Me? I've got lots of friends."

"Oh?"

"Sure."

Then he says, "You know what's wrong with the world today?"

"No. What?"

"We've lost contact with nature. Not only the real world of grass and trees and lakes and streams, but *our* nature. We've lost touch with ourselves and each other. We stopped sharing; stopped telling each other what it's really like. . ."

His big watery eyes never seem to blink. And it's like I'm transparent and he sees my spine. I get up and prowl the gloomy cage. Old Dub kind of wilts across the bunk.

"Little lies don't hurt other people much," he says. "But watch out when you lie to yourself."

This wasted old guy is an archaeologist: he's read the hieroglyphics in my secret caves. Behind me a key clicks in the lock. A big gray man motions me forward.

"Come on, kid. Your dad's here."

This big guy is the size of a small train and he's wondering why I hang back . . .

Dad is out there: Dad the Mature; Dad the Strong; Dad the Boss. I scratch my head. Can a father *fire* his own son?

7

In the front seat of a senile Ford, the silence is thick as mumps. The big moon teases above the treetops and I wish I was on it. When I can't take the silence anymore, I say:

"I'm sorry, Dad."

"That's not good enough."

I seethe a little in the dark. The least he can do is accept my apology. And I can't think of a single adult reply.

(It's difficult to describe my dad. I've always thought he looked like a big idea: a big idea in a small man's clothes. He's not much larger than I am, and I'm not the world's largest.

(I always thought he hid behind things, too: like the steering wheel that night, and his horn-rim glasses and his pipe. And I *know* he had a habit of hiding behind his newspaper.)

When I think I'm under control, I say:

"What do you mean it's not good enough?"

He goes right on, as though I'm a page he's turned.

"You're lucky. She won't prefer charges . . . You know how it starts, Jory?"

"What?"

"Crime."

"How?"

"With small things. Carelessness. Not caring what you do or who you hurt or what the results are."

"I'm not a criminal."

"You acted like one tonight. It's hard to deny that we *are* what we act like."

I'm limp as noodles. I don't care. I've tried to talk to him before about lots of things. We may live in the same house, but our rooms are in different orbits.

"OK. So I'm a criminal."

"Being flip won't help."

"I don't know what to *do*. I said I was sorry. You want me to sit in jail?"

"Of course not."

We're home now and I get out to raise the garage door. He drives inside and for a minute we stand like strangers in the half-darkened garage.

". . . What I want you to do is the very best you *can* do. That's quite a lot, you know?"

"Is it?"

He reaches out like he's going to touch my arm and then he waves me ahead of him. I'm wondering what he'd say to Reve. Reve the handsome; Reve the victorious . . .

The kitchen lights are yellowmellow. Mom's all ivory with a touch of her own light. She's pouring me a glass of milk when I walk in. She kind of goes all soft and gives me one of those smiles of hers. It gets to me so much that I leave the room.

I used to catch myself looking at my mother a lot, but I made myself stop. I was afraid I embarrassed her. For one thing, she's kind of shy.

There's a music in my mother you can almost see—the way she moves and does things. She's the only person I know who can make doing the laundry seem elegant.

I go on up to my room and shut the door. All I want is to turn off the lights and be a tree for about two weeks. And I'm thinking about that poor dumb dog lying in the ditch . . .

But Mom comes in with two sandwiches and a glass of milk. She says nothing at first, just leans against my desk and touches a small globe of the world and makes it turn.

"Were you bored, Jory, or what?"

"I don't know."

"Were you mad about something?"

"Not really."

"Was it something *we've* done?"

"It was just—a crazy stunt."

". . . I guess I could play twenty questions, but you'd outshrug me."

If my bed was a boat, I'd be rowing into the dark. What Dad says is in his voice. With Mom it's more her eyes: it's like being under a microscope.

"Jory . . . Have you thought much about what you want to be someday?"

"Oh, a man of the world, I guess."

I didn't give that much thought. It just came out. And compared to her voice, mine sounds like static.

"You know what I'd like you to be?"

"No."

"A man with a great spirit . . . Laughter is great, Jory. It's like practicing—for life."

She drifts over and grazes my forehead with one elegant finger. When she's gone I feel so dumb I want to get up and give myself an F at least eight feet high—in colors that glow in the dark.

8

As surely as there were half Crazies and real Crazies, there were real days and there were Sundays—half days. On Sunday I always seemed to be in limbo between what I'd done and what I might do, between the fantasies of Saturday night and the hard facts of Monday morning.

That Sunday was like the tenth inning of a tough baseball game. From the time I was up, I was caught in a squeeze play between home and third. My conscience bothered me.

All day I think about it, but I wait until dark. Asking for the car's like getting the keys to Fort Knox. I tell Dad I want to go apologize to Miss Elkins.

"Can't you call her?"

"Aw, Dad, it's not the same on the phone."

"OK. But don't stay long."

So I'm a big, fat liar, but I've got to get it off my mind. In a jiff, I'm streaking out of town on the old highway. It takes a while, but I find the dog, a pale lump in the dark.

It's gross handling it, but I get the carcass into a

pasteboard box and put it in the trunk. I turn the car around and head back.

With the lights off, I ease up the alley behind our house. It takes longer to dig the grave than I thought it would. Finally I lower the dog into the hole and cover it up, first with dirt, then with leaves and stuff.

So it's there beside my dog, the one that got run over, too. And a squirrel some dumb kid killed and left on the sidewalk. Plus a frog, two sparrows, and a garter snake.

Hands in pockets, I shrug and eye the bright stars. The sky's an undiscovered paradise and there I am collecting carcasses.

I put the car away and take Dad the keys. I'm glad he's hiding behind the Sunday paper.

So I think: That's it. My conscience is clear. But in the hall upstairs, I pass Reve's room. For a minute a picture in my mind almost comes into focus. Then it's gone. Yet I stand for a while inside my door with the lights off.

9

By a side door I enter the hallowed halls of Marshal Senior High. Jory the Great's got a smile for everybody. I cat-walk down the hall toward my locker.

Maybe I'll write an exposé on the halls of Marshal High. Business as usual: One guy's slipping another three joints rolled in notebook paper. Louie the dealer. The stuff is everywhere.

I tried it a few times and it went to my head. Suddenly I had the brain of a zonked gorilla. I saw things: hairy trees and bloody sidewalks. So I leave it alone and that goes for the watered-down speed you can get anytime.

I duck in the boy's room and already the place is filling up with smoke. I'm combing my hair and a couple of guys come up.

"Hey, man, you dudes really take that car?"

"Sure," I say. "Brand-new Buick."

"Cool," the other says.

On the way to class, Coach Pelham stops me. I'm waiting for him to mention the car.

"What do you hear from Reve?" he says.

"He's doin' OK."

"I heard he made the regimental baseball team."

"Yeah."

"He ought to be an inspiration for you, Jory—a brother like that."

Then I'm there alone by the water fountain and the hall's almost empty. I'm inspired all right. With my hand on the spigot, I shoot a stream five feet high.

10

Midafternoon: senior English in a warm, crowded room with bad air. Outside the trees are friendly and sun-spangled. I envy the flag, dancing on the flagpole. All around there's a dull, shuffling sound: a restless army eager to take on soft drinks and french fries.

The teacher's getting us psyched up for a theme: *What's Fun?* she wants us to write about. She's asking one of the guys what fun means to him.

"I'm easy to please," he says. "Ask Jory."

Most of the class laughs and it's a good laugh. When the bell rings, I'm surrounded; I'm a celebrity. Then everyone's gone but Elena. Elena Huerta.

"Don't let it go to your head," she says. "They change heroes often."

Her deep-brown eyes are like a deer's: soft with light in them. I think I'm gawking too long and I turn away.

Elena's Spanish-American—Chicano. Her mind's quick and keen. It cuts through b.s. and doubletalk and she says what she thinks. Maybe that's why she's not very popular. She's kind of round, too. Some of the guys started calling her Doughnut. The name stuck and I always thought it unfair.

When I turn around, she's gone. Just vanished. I keep thinking of those eyes. Then Bud's there with a serious crease in his pudding face.

"I tried to find that old dog," he says.

"When?"

"Early this morning before school. I drove out there. It was gone. I was going to bury it."

"I guess the trash people found it."

"Doesn't it bother you at all?"

"*Me?*" I say. "What's a dumb dog?"

Keep moving, moving, moving, that was the idea. Bud and I head for a Coke when school's out. It's a long walk downtown to Pete's, along a street crowded with fast-food joints. When my legs slow, my head keeps going.

Everything's Taco something these days: Taco Bell, Taco Grande, Taco Tico . . . Taco Tacky, I think: Tricky Taco, Tic-Tac-Taco, Whacko Taco, Stucco Taco, Taco Puko.

Same with hamburgers: *Be the first in your neighborhood to have a golden arch . . .* And E-Z-Burger, Royal Burger, Burger King, and Whataburger. Bud and I make up our own:

Sleazy Burger. Teasy Burger. E-Gad-a-Burger. I-Gotta-Burger. You-Gotta-Burger . . . He-Ain't-Got-No-Burger . . .

"How 'bout a Burger-of-the-Month Club," I say, "from all over the world . . . Boliviaburger. Zanzibarburger. Johannesburger . . ."

"Got one for you," Bud says.

"What?"

"Iceburger."

The streets are *real* Crazies: the sky is full of signs winking like idiots in the sunlight . . . Quik-Stop, Launder-eze, Sav-Mor, Wash-n-Glo, Eat-n-Run, Gas-R-Up, Bowl Rite . . .

"Hey, Bud. You ever wonder why we can't spell?"

"You have to learn to *read* first."

Cars are something else, too. First of all you need a gas mask. It would help to be armed, too. The streets swarm with Barracudas, Hornets, Cougars, Wildcats, Gremlins, and Cobras. If they don't get you, the Darts and Lancers will.

"You know what?" I tell Bud. "*Real* Crazies grow up and work in Detroit—naming cars."

Then I wonder: What am I getting so upset about? Before I can answer, a picture winks in the back of my mind like a neon sign.

11

The days fly by like kites let loose. It's almost dark when I leave the house. Wearing gym clothes, I'm racing down the street toward the high-school stadium. At night when no one's around, I have my own Olympics.

I streak like a champion and thousands cheer from the stands as Jory breaks all records. I've made about two laps when I see the coach coming toward me, and I slow down. Sometimes he keeps the baseball team after dark.

"Jory, you've got real speed. How come you never ran for me?"

"I don't know."

"Oh, come on. You'd shrug off an earthquake. Is it Reve? Is it just because Reve—"

"Who could compete against *his* record? He won everything."

"Except the Science Prize."

"I forgot about that."

"That remark I made the other day—about inspiration. I didn't mean to embarrass you."

"I can take it."

"When you get to college, you ought to try for the track team."

"Maybe I will."

"Hope so. Goodnight."

"Night."

I'm running again and I'm mad as a Hornet/Cobra/Gremlin and I run all the harder. I think I'm about to explode. I glance up and there's a small flicker of light, like a match, from the top of the stadium.

Someone's up there, watching, and it's kind of spooky. I think it might be the coach, but I'm sure I saw him leave in his car . . . I look again and the shadow's gone . . . Maybe I was just seeing things.

All the way home, I keep my speed up. After I've showered I sit at my desk, staring at homework. The full moon's a weird, blue-white blossom in the sky. I think about the Science Prize. That's about the only thing that Reve never won.

There's not much time left, but I think I can win it. I can draw well, and I'll do something really great: I'll design a city: a city of the future; a city on the moon.

There won't be any dumb neon signs cluttering up the sky. And no dumb cars prowling around, cluttering up the streets. Not even a Trans Am.

The city will be built under giant geodesic domes. Parks will blossom everywhere, busy with swans and ducks and even peacocks. One thing there won't be for sure: not one single dumb graveyard.

I've made two or three drawings and it's going pretty well. Then I'm thinking about that shadow up there in the stadium, wondering if it's just in my head like the other stuff . . .

12

Weeks have passed. I'm drooping around school like a melted Hershey. I've been staying up late working on my Moon City project and it shows. This particular day we're herding into the locker room after gym class. It's not my favorite place.

Today it's hot and loud and guys are chasing each other and having wet-towel fights. I find a quiet corner and begin to undress. I'm sitting there wilting and this guy leans over.

"Hey, Hall. How come you never horse around like the other guys?"

"I'm not a horse," I say.

Whatever reputation I had as a cool dude seems to be gone. Elena was right: they *do* change heroes.

On the wall beside me is a trophy case. Every other one seems to have the same name: Reve Hall. *Reve Hall.* REVE HALL. Why doesn't the coach hire a plane and write it in the sky?

I go over to the punching bag and I give it all I've got—first with one hand, then the other. Then I'm actually beating on it with both hands. I stop. One knuckle is bleeding. I go over and sit on a bench and I stare at that little trickle of blood.

And like it's yesterday, I'm twelve and I'm coming home from school. It's November, with gray frozen trees and the air's just cold enough to make you feel alive all over. I'm happy as stars for no special reason, and when I get within a block of the house I start calling Mutt.

Mutt is a little black and white dog I found two years before, and he's always there when I come home. But he's not there that day and I come on up the street and I see something lying out there on the pavement and I can't believe it.

He doesn't seem hurt or anything, except for a small trickle of blood out of his mouth on his white fur.

First I run: I just take off running and I've gone four or five blocks and I stop. I know I have to go back. So I go back and find a pasteboard box and put him inside and I bury him in the back yard.

I don't say anything, I just bury him, and I put a little stone there on top of the fresh earth. (And I don't know it then but that's the start of a neighborhood graveyard) . . .

So I'm sitting there in the locker room and I'm *seventeen years old,* wondering what the heck I'm thinking about *that* for. It's quiet now; everyone's gone. I've put on my clothes without even knowing it.

On the way out, I pass the shower room. There's a window way up high and the sun is slanting through that window—a molten bar of pale gold. It's like church or something, and I reach in and turn on one of the showers. Now the water's a fountain, and a silver mist is drifting up through the shaft of gold sunlight.

Then I do something I've always wanted to do: I step in the shower with all my clothes on. The water is cold and it feels great and I'm really digging it.

I get out and stand there dripping on the floor, and I'm about fifty degrees cooler. I look wild in the mirror, but I like it. And the coach comes in.

"Jory . . . What's going on?"

"Nothin'."

"How'd you get wet?"

"In the shower."

"With all your clothes on?"

"Yes."

"In the *shower?*"

"Well, it didn't rain in here."

Frowning, the coach touches his forehead a couple of times with his fist.

"You *on* anything?" he asks.

"No."

". . . I don't get it. Whatever made you do a thing like that?"

"Look. So, I got wet. What's the big deal?"

"You've changed, Jory. Ever since you and Bud stole that car, you've been—"

"We borrowed it."

"You *took* something that wasn't yours."

"And we *took* it back."

"I don't want to argue with you."

"Good. Let's don't."

". . . I guess you know I'll have to tell your folks about this."

"No, I don't understand why you *have* to."

"That's not an ordinary thing to do."

"OK, so I'm not ordinary."

"All right, now, settle down. Watch your tone."

"My *tone?* Man, what is this, anyway? I just had one of the best times I've had in months. I got a little wet. Big damn deal."

I start to walk away and he grabs my shoulder. I mean he really grabs it; his fingers are like claws. Everything considered, I think I am cool as January. I turn around real slow and eyeball his hand.

"Might pick on someone your own size," I say.

He lets me go and I stalk out. I want to go somewhere besides home, so I make it down some back streets and head into the park. I sit a long time in the sunlight and dry out. On the lagoon the swans are so peaceful I want to be one.

13

Like Buddha himself, Dad's waiting on the front steps, all self-contained and full of wisdom. Inscrutable.

He glances up as I cut across the front yard: Clint the Cat is walking like Louie the Limper. Dad's cleaning his pipe and I wish I had one to clean. My hands seem a foot long and I shove them in my pockets.

Buddha is about to speak: I can always tell when he adjusts his glasses. So I think: I'll get the jump on him. I'll get into it first.

I sit beside him and now my hands are trapped, as though they're thoughts, in my pockets. *What was I going to say?*

"Run you a race," is what comes out.

"What?"

"Race you around the block."

He manages the shadow of a smile, and I think: It's going to be OK.

"I'll say one thing," he tells me, "you are about six feet of pure surprise."

"Is that bad?"

"No. Not yet . . ."

There's something ominous about that, like the thick gray clouds hanging over one edge of the city.

"Did Coach call?"

"Yes . . ."

"Dad, I just—I was feeling kind of down. I don't know, I guess I think too much. Anyway, it was—just a spur of the moment thing. Impulse. I'd always wanted to do that—just climb in there with all my clothes on. It was just a stunt, see?"

"Coach Pelham says you—well, you're not like yourself."

"I'm all right."

"You sure? There's nothing really—"

"I'm fine."

"That stunt, as you call it. It's not exactly—normal."

"What's normal?"

"What?"

"I said, 'What's normal?' I mean, can't you just be yourself sometimes? Can't you be—spontaneous?"

"Sure . . . The coach thinks your attitude's been bad for quite a while. He can't understand why you yelled at him. Why did you?"

"Why did he make such a thing out of it? He could have—laughed."

"You could have, too."

Dad studies me for so long I turn away and try to whistle. I can't.

"Jory . . . You're not—taking anything?"

"You mean drugs?"

"Yes."

"How many times do I have to tell you? No!"

". . . It's just—the incident in the shower. Oh, I know it's no big thing, but there's the car, too. Bill thought, well, both incidents were the kinds of things, you know, a guy might do if he was taking something."

"I'll make a public statement. We'll have it notarized. I'll get on TV. I'll—"

"Son . . . Don't fight *me*."

He sighs; his voice drops. It gets kind of soft—real concerned—and that's harder to deal with than being mad at him. He says:

"You know, I've seen a difference in you since Reve left. Reve has, too. We just got a letter and he said you don't even write him anymore."

The mention of Reve causes a short circuit, and I'm flushed all over. It's like something comes down over my eyes, and I can't see well. Then I'm standing and waving my arms.

"I made one mistake," I say, "one really dumb mistake—taking that car—and everyone thinks I'm a criminal—or a drug addict."

"Come on," Dad says, "lower your voice."

"You wouldn't think that about Reve. You just wouldn't do it."

He gives me the funniest look, as though he doesn't know who I am. I go in the house and storm up the stairs. For a while I lay on the bed feeling sorry for myself, and I get to thinking: How dumb can you get?

It's thundering outside and I walk around the house, kicking sticks out of the way. The air's special—supercharged, like just before a big football game—and already I can smell the rain. A big leaf flutters down and I pick it up and take it inside. They're just sitting down to eat and I ease over to the table. I lay the leaf down; then I slowly turn it over.

I'm turning over a new leaf, I say.

14

A golden Saturday: the sun's a bold lion and Tiger Jory's on the way to meet Bud downtown. We're planning a camping trip. I take the long way around and go through the park.

I'm feeling great. The Moon City project is really coming along. I'll not only win the Science Prize, I might even make the cover of *Time.*

The park is a carnival of green with small kids everywhere loud and bright and there's even a man selling balloons. I buy a big orange one and then I don't know what to do with it.

I'm walking along the edge of the lagoon, digging my handsome reflection. The balloon drifts over my shoulder like an extra sun. Ahead, Cara Reed is sitting by herself near the water.

She doesn't see me and I think of turning around and going the other way. She's going through a rough time and I'm afraid I don't have anything to say.

(Cara's dad is in the hospital. He's an alcoholic and he's been in and out of hospitals a dozen times. I've heard he might die this time.)

So I'm already going the other way, but I glance back over my shoulder. She's alone. She's really alone.

Jory the Great saunters up and says hello.

"Hi, Jory."

I sit beside her and I've got this dumb balloon and I don't know where to put it.

"Want a balloon?" I say.

"No, thanks."

"How 'bout some gum? It's sugarless."

"No . . ."

It seems an hour passes and I can't think of one intelligent remark. I'm actually sweating and out of the blue I'm asking her to go to the prom with me.

"Are you serious?"

"Sure."

"You're not just asking because—"

"I'm asking because I want to take you."

"I'm not sure—what's going to happen. Can I let you know?"

"OK."

Now I'm really stuck and it's hot as borrowed cars and I think I'm gonna bust or something so I let the balloon go. We both watch it go up and up and up.

"Why'd you do that?" she says.

"I don't know."

But I do: it's like the swans on the water—free. Free, free, free . . .

Bud is waiting in Pete's and the place is worse than usual. It's the color of *chewed* cigars. I need sonar to get through the smoke.

"One of these days," I say, "they'll have to use dynamite to clear this air."

"What's wrong with you anyway?" Bud asks.

"I don't like smoke."

"It's not just that. The other day it was signs—and cars. Then it was hamburger joints."

"Wouldn't want my sister to marry one."

"You *love* hamburgers."

"A nice place to visit, but—"

"What's bugging you, man?"

"I don't know."

"You oughta have the biggest shoulders in town."

"Why?"

"You shrug enough."

". . . We going on the camping trip?"

"Sure."

"Day after the prom?"

"Yeah. Dad said I could have the car . . . You got a date for the prom?"

"Of course."

"Who with?"

"Cara Reed."

"Didn't know you knew her."

"I didn't either."

"Now what's that mean?"

"It means—"

That was one of the few times I recall having no answer, not even a bluff. That was also the day, I believe, that I added the next-to-last casualty to my backyard collection—a horned toad, lying on its back in the park.

At home I put it with the menagerie in the yard. I stared at the small grave.

Only kids do stuff like this, I said to myself . . . Picking up dumb, hurt, dead things . . .

Yet I still had a feeling for those things, just beneath the surface—a confused, changeable feeling like I had toward Reve.

Already the moon was up. I wanted to howl—a teenage werewolf in the world's smallest graveyard. Having nothing better to do, I laughed.

15

Upstairs in a downstairs mood I'm trying to write Reve a letter. I can't even write a salutation, so I make faces in the mirror—Clint the Cat and Jory the Great—then I'm staring at it. My eyes look funny: they say *tilt*.

(First I think maybe because I got my wires crossed at school. After gym class this guy comes up:

("Hey, Hall, when're you gonna take another one of your famous showers?")

I make another start on the letter. *Dear Reve* doesn't sound right.

Hey, Reve, I write, *how's it going?*

I cross that out, too.

Hiya, Reve. What's happening?

I'm not the type that says "Hiya." In fact, I don't think anybody says "Hiya" anymore. Maybe Sandra Dee in one of those creaky TV movies.

I know what I want to tell Reve, but *will* I?

I couldn't even swim until Reve taught me how. He taught me just about everything I know. I learned how to pitch a tent and set a trout line and clean fish and play tennis and—

Then he's getting ready to leave: just like that he's going into the marines . . .

The night Dad took him to the bus, he came into my room, and I'd decided not to speak to him.

"What's the matter?" he says.

"You know what's wrong. We were going on a camping trip up in the mountains. We were going to stay a week and fish all day and—"

"Hey, man, I've got my own life to live. I can't hang around here forever."

"Go on then. Who cares?"

"I'll be back in a few weeks, after basic training. Maybe we can take a trip then."

"You promised, Reve. People shouldn't say things they don't mean."

"I know. I'm sorry . . . But I've been thinking about the Corps a long time, you know that. I decided this was the time to join. Can't you understand?"

"No."

". . . Look, I've gotta go. Dad's waiting. Don't you want to shake hands?"

He's standing there with his hand out and I turn away.

"OK, Buddy. Take care. See you soon."

So he's gone and I lie there a few seconds and I hear the car start. Then I'm tearing down the stairs and out the front door and the car's already a half block away. I run after it, yelling:

"Reve! Reve, come back. Wait a minute."

The car stops and Dad backs up. Reve gets out of the car and runs toward me.

"Hey, man, don't get all upset. What is it?"

I'm out of breath and I start gasping: "Its—I—something I need—to tell you."

"Go on, then. Tell me."

"I—well—it was the other night and—. . ."

"Yeah? I'm listening."

And then I know I can't tell him: I don't have the guts. But he's there, waiting, and I have to say something.

"It's nothin', Reve. Honest."

"You sure?"

"Yeah. I just—wanted to say goodbye like—like a man."

I stick out my hand and he takes it and he starts to put his arm around me and I move back and then he's gone.

Going back to the house, I don't feel like a man; I feel like a liar.

And I still feel like a liar sitting up there in my room. Because there was something I wanted to tell my brother—something I needed to tell . . .

That's why my eyes say tilt. I've got this stuff inside me and I can't tell anyone and it's growing in there. Like one of those big wobbly knots you see on trees, it's growing inside. So I try again on paper:

> *Reve,*
> *Made general yet? Bet it won't take long. Anyway, I hope you have lots of fun and win lots of medals.*
>
> *Maybe when you get out, we can do something together—start a business or just travel around.*
>
> *But before you come back, there's something you ought to know. It was a couple of nights before you left. I*

I wad the paper up and throw it away. I can't tell him, not even in a letter.

Downstairs I try to cool it for a while. But I forget it's ten o'clock—Obituary Hour on TV. This nerd with a smile comes on to tell us who died—and how—throughout the whole world.

I'm thinking: *Blood-a-burger* . . . *Car-Wreck-a-burger* . . . *Murderburger*.

Real Crazies grow up and get on national TV.

I think about sending the world a cheer-up telegram of about ten thousand words—collect.

16

Jory the Great is cat-walking down the crowded hall looking for Cara. Faces float past: happysad, veryglad, partly-
bad faces. The prom is two days away and I'm still up in
the air about a date. Somebody calls:

"Hey, Jory. Had a shower lately?"

I look neither right nor left; I didn't hear a thing. Stiff-
upper-lipped Captain Jory slips through a sea of strangers.
Cara's adrift by her locker and I make myself smile.

"Hi."

"Hi," she says, and there are dark circles beneath her
eyes.

"It's, you know, getting kind of late and I thought I'd—
check with you."

"Jory . . . That was really nice of you, but—I really
don't want to go to the prom."

"It might—well—make you feel better."

"Thanks, anyway."

"Is your dad—OK?"

"No."

"Well . . . I hope he is—soon."

"Thanks."

Then I'm walking away, thinking: The least she could have done is give me a little notice.

Quick as bad news I'm mad again. It's getting so the least little thing sets me off. I slouch on toward my next class and the thing is I *know* what's bugging me. I just don't know what to do about it.

Mr. Willard's checking roll outside the door to history class. He likes to wear blue and green together and he doesn't have enough hair to comb, but he's a nice guy anyway.

"Jory."

"Yes."

"What do you hear from Reve?"

"Nothin' much."

"I heard he was the best marksman in his entire company."

"Yeah. I forgot about that."

"That guy can do anything. He was the only student who ever made a perfect score on the American history final."

"Like you say, he can do anything."

"Tell him hello for me."

"Sure."

When I sit across from Bud, I slam my books down on the chair arm.

"What's wrong?" he says.

"I don't know," I say.

But I do.

17

Coach Pelham once said that guilt, unrestrained and not dealt with, could drive a person crazy. That stuck with me, because I was always kind of interested in craziness—the degrees of it each of us had, and the different forms it took.

Today I believe there are two very common forms of madness, and at seventeen, I was suffering from both of them:

(1) the inability to profit from past mistakes;

(2) presuming to know what goes on in another's mind.

And I'd always been interested in whatever it was that kept one person from going off the deep end—and made the other plunge all the way down. Chance? Fate? Luck? God?

I didn't know. And I didn't think about God much. That's kind of like thinking about madness: you usually don't do it until you have to.

At school and at home, some of my guidelines were getting blurred. I was convinced that my parents disapproved of me generally, though I couldn't be specific. Into their most casual looks, I read the most complex of criticism.

And *was* I a fairly average guy that the other seniors kind of liked, or was I on the edge of things—an outsider like Ellie—the object of sleazy humor?

It was getting so I didn't even recognize myself in the mirror. Mirrors were magic, I decided; they changed. Every day they made me look different.

Another thing about guilt. Let it pile up enough, it performs magic, too: it turns into fear.

Over the past weeks, as I'd grown less sure of myself, I grew less comfortable with my surroundings. First I was only critical of people and things. Then slowly—the way shadows move in at sunset—I began to fear them.

It's a warm night, kind of cloudy. Still. I stand outside our house, listening: it's *so* still. I wait, expecting a noise of some kind. But what?

Trotting, I head down toward the stadium, past familiar houses and neighbors that wave. But something's not quite right—is it me or them? Twice I stop and look back, thinking that I'm being followed.

It's a relief to get to the stadium. I feel safer somehow behind the locked gate and the twelve-foot steel fence. But: *Safer from WHAT?*

  . . . Bears, boogie men, Frankenstein, Dracula? . . . What is it, Jory? You scared of the dark?

(And though I could not have admitted it then, that was very close to the truth: I *was* afraid of the dark. The dark was all nights without stars; all days without sunlight; all that existed *beyond* shadow, and all that unexplored terrain in the familiar but foreign head of Jory Hall.)

But I'm running well now on the cinder track. Muscles loosen and stretch; I move easier. I've got that pumped-up feeling and I get a second wind.

The crazy little pictures flash in my head, but I'm flying now: piston-kneed, air-cooled, streamlined, super-charged Jory the Great.

. . . First I'll finish the Moon City project. There's no doubt it will win the Science Prize. And *that* prize will attract scholarships and offers from all the best schools. I'll pick one out. I'll make the track team—any team . . .

A flashing picture is still in the back of my mind, but I ignore it. I could outrun anything tonight—anything! Barracudas, Cobras, Sherman tanks, The Bomb—bring 'em all on!

It's like a brief exultation and I glance up toward the sky and I slow. It moves up there just enough that I can't ignore it. It's not a mirage or a bad thought or a fantasy: it won't go away.

Panting like crazy, I come to a stop. There *is* someone up there, just standing in the dark, watching me. *Like I watched Reve*, I'm thinking, but the connection blurs, fades.

Now the shadow moves, without a sound, along the top of the stadium. For a moment it hesitates then it goes down a ramp inside the stadium.

I stand there a long time until I'm almost cool. It was like God up there watching: watching Jory the Great try and outrun the world.

18

The night of the prom: the entire senior class is celebrating like it's New Year's Eve, and I'm up in my room having Halloween. It's eight-thirty and if I kill more time, the prom will be over. On a clean piece of paper I've just started a new drawing for Moon City when Mom calls:

"Jory, it's getting late. Where are you?"

I don't want her to think I'm *completely* nuts so I get dressed and go downstairs. She fusses with the collar of my jacket. Her fingers touch the back of my neck and I shy away.

"Jory . . . You don't feel badly about not having a date, do you?"

"No."

I'm getting to be the biggest liar in the entire state. To avoid her, I stop in front of a mirror and comb my hair again for the fifth time.

Mom says: "Seems just like yesterday Reve was going to the senior prom. He won a dance contest that night. They gave him a small, sterling silver medal and—"

"I know. I know. He could do anything, right?"

"What?"

"I'm sorry, Mom."

"Did I upset you?"

"It's not you, it's me. I . . . ."

She's walked over close and I think maybe she can see my thoughts written all over my face. So I turn real quick and give her a phony smile and I bolt for the door.

I'm running down the street, picking up speed, trees flashing past, and I cross Elm Avenue and this guy screeches his car to a halt and yells out the window and I keep going. (A Gremlin, no doubt.)

Finally I'm out of breath and I think: Man, this is stupid. What're you runnin for? But I don't even slow down. I keep right on until I see the high school. In the dark it looks like a shoe factory. Some real heels in there, too, I think.

But I can hear the music now and my heart's pounding like the drum inside. I stroll into the parking lot and lean on a blue Camaro, a polished jewel in the moonlight.

One of these days I'll have a new car. That'll turn some heads—that blue Trans Am, maybe. People will know me and they'll—

Jory the Great, I say aloud, and head for the gym where the action is. From the big open doorway I can see all the crowded dance floor. In the flashing light from the bandstand, the girls in party dresses whirl and float like butterflies. I wonder where my net is . . .

Bud's out there having a great time and doesn't see me wave. Mr. Willard's doing the hustle with the English teacher. Coach Pelham looks right at me and I crane my neck as though I've lost my date.

Back against one wall I hustle the punch bowl: orange stuff, kind of sweet, kind of sour, with fresh fruit floating in it. I've got my nose in a paper cup when Elena appears from nowhere. She looks great in a pale blue dress with her hair pulled back.

"*Que pasa?*" she says.

"Nada."

Those big round eyes are another country: *el sol y agua y estrellas y luna y noche . . .*

"Are you with anyone?"

"No. Are you?"

"No. You want to dance?"

"Muchisimo."

Just as we're getting out on the floor, the music stops. The next number is slow and I'm glad. She's a really good dancer; she has a light touch. Jory the Great has two dumbbells for feet. When we're headed back toward the punch bowl, she says:

"You can call me Ellie."

"Just call me JG."

"G?"

"A little joke. Stands for Jory the Great. I like to kid myself."

"People *should* think of themselves as great."

"I wish I did."

"Why don't you?"

I shrug, and I'm thinking: Jory, you'll get in the *Guinness Book of World Records* yet—for shrugging.

"You want to enter the dance contest, Jory?"

"I ought to enter the shrug contest."

She's laughing and I like the sound—light, musical, like high piano notes. Then this girl that's in our class comes up and says:

"Elena, someone wants to see you outside."

"Me? Who is it?"

"He didn't say."

I don't know why but I glance toward the door and a couple of jocks—real Burt Reynolds types—are watching us and they grin and disappear outside.

Ellie says, "I'll be back in a minute."

So I have some more punch, and I'm really uncomfortable. Something isn't right, and I head for the door. Outside there's no one around, but I hear Ellie's voice.

"I don't want to go *anywhere* with you!"

She's standing with the two jocks over by the blue Camaro. She whirls and starts back toward the gym and one guy grabs her wrist.

"Come on, Doughnut. Don't play hard to get."

She jerks away from him.

"I *am* hard to get."

She's moving away again and one guy steps in front of her. They're standing between two parked cars and now she's blocked. I run toward them, yelling:

"Leave her alone!"

"Look who's here," one of them says.

"Go take a shower, Hall."

I rush at one guy and push him in the chest and he goes back against the car. Then I swing at the other guy and just barely graze his shoulder. He hits me twice and I go down and see stars in the asphalt.

"You're out of your league, Hall," one of them says, and they walk away.

My nose is bleeding and my pants are torn where my knee hit the paving. I don't want Ellie to see me, but she's bending down with a handkerchief.

"I'll just mess it up," I say.

"Go on. That's what handkerchiefs are for."

I kind of clean up my face and I stand.

"Are you hurt anyplace else?"

"I'm OK."

(I'm glad you can't see ego.)

"I'll replace the handkerchief."

"Forget it . . . Let's go back. We'll act like nothing happened."

"I'll—I'll see you."

"Wait! . . . Where you going?"

"I don't know. Just—around."

"Can I come along?"

"I'm not very good company."

"I disagree."

We walk along, quiet as books. I think about braille.

We're in the nice, old residential part of town, and Ellie says:

"I wish we lived here."

"I do, too. We'd almost be neighbors."

"We live in a small house."

"On South Street, isn't it?"

"Um-hmm. You know that part of town?"

"Kinda."

It's a sad part of town with square frame houses peeling like sunburns. Trash cans run over in the streets. Abandoned cars park in front yards, and old refrigerators lean on dirty porches.

(Where Ellie lived was another thing I didn't want to think about. That was before I began to understand that you have to deal with things in some way. If you don't, they deal with you.)

"I bet you're an only child," Ellie says.

"I have one brother."

"I have four—and three sisters."

"That's a lot."

Jory, I think you are brilliant. Your conversation sparkles like dishwater.

19

The park swirls with greenery and coolness. Already I feel better, and I'm glad she's telling me things—personal things. I think maybe I'll be honest with her, too. I'll tell her what's been bugging me for months.

But we stroll over to the lagoon and the moon's a plump pearl in the dark-green water. It's like a scene from a movie; only the music is missing. If I tell her what I'm really like, I'm afraid I'll turn her off. So I whistle the swans a tune . . .

"Jory . . ."

"Yeah."

"That was a special thing you did, charging those guys."

"I didn't do so hot."

"It was the idea . . . You know something else?"

"What?"

"I knew you kind of liked me."

"How?"

"I can tell the way people stare. Some people turn off 'cause my skin is different."

"I like your color."

"I know . . . Can you imagine God looking down on the whole Earth and saying: How *dare* you not like the colors of all my people! Colors are to enjoy . . ."

"Some people are—dumb."

"And cruel. But they pay for that. I think people pay for what's inside."

I feel kind of spooky, as though she's reading my mind.

"Look," I say. "You want to go back to the dance?"

"I'd rather be here . . . Are you really designing a city for the moon?"

"Just some drawings. How'd you know?"

"Bud told me . . . I bet you'll be famous some day."

"*Me?*"

"I bet you will."

"You must be thinking of my brother. Reve's the one who can do anything. Me, I'm just ordinary."

"I don't think so. Ordinary people don't plan whole cities for another planet. And I bet you win the Science Prize. Bud thinks so, too."

"I'd like to win *something*. My brother won everything he tried."

"*My* brother would win the grouch prize. I don't think John likes anything—but me, maybe. He thinks I'm special."

"You *are* special."

"You think I'm fat?"

"No."

"Tell the truth."

"I don't—you're round."

"That's another word for fat."

"No, it's not. Round is kind of—full. Round things—people—are smooth, and soft-looking."

". . . I'm going on a diet this summer."

"Maybe I will, too. I'd like to gain ten pounds."

"I'll loan them to you."

"You look fine the way you are."

"So do you."

On the other side of the water, I think I see some-thing move. A sick feeling goes all through me. Then I'm thinking: Man, what is *wrong* with you? I look again. Only fragments of streetlight play through the rustling trees.

Ellie lies back on the grass and even in the semidark her eyes have that special glow. I stretch out beside her, and the stars—the *stars:* dazzling in space like points in the future.

I'm touching the grass with my fingers and then I'm touching her hand and I close my fingers around her small hand, and we're two astronauts gliding through space . . .

"Jory . . . Remember what President Kennedy said? Mr. Willard quoted it in history class."

"I'm not sure."

"He said: 'Don't tell me how it is. I *know* that. Tell me how it could be.' "

"I remember."

"I'm glad you're designing a city for the future. Tell us how it could be, Jory. Tell the world . . ."

And Jory the Great drifts up through the stars with his girl. When they land on the moon, thousands cheer and lights blaze in the giant dome of the city he's de-signed: a city of peace and light.

Far below, the world watches on its TV sets, and the word goes out: Jory Hall for President. Jory for President of the Universe.

I'm amazed at how quickly you can get high in your own mind—and low. For I lean up on one elbow as something moves. I was right. Someone's over there, near the big tree, watching us. It's a thin shadow, male, I think. Whatever it is, it's coming toward us.

20

"Ellie!"

She has fallen asleep. Now she stirs; her eyes open wide, startled.

"What is it?"

"Someone's over there in the shadows, near the bend in the water. He's coming this way. Get ready to run."

I connect it with the figure in the stadium. Some nut— a real Crazy—maybe freaked out on drugs. I can almost see his face now. He stops.

"John," Ellie says.

The shadow says something in Spanish and Ellie answers. He's glaring at me and Ellie moves between us.

"John, this is Jory."

"What're you doing here?" he says. "I looked everywhere."

"We were talking," Ellie says. "We got tired of the dance. We took a walk and—"

"You know what time it is?"

"No."

"It's one-thirty in the morning."

"I guess we dozed off," I say.

He glares again and I decide that it's better not to say anything.

"Come on, Ellie," he says. "Mama's worried. You're an hour late."

"All right. But don't blame Jory. He's a friend . . . Good night, Jory. Thanks for everything."

"Night."

Tall, glaring John steps closer.

"That's a bad thing, keeping my sister out late."

"I'm sorry. I didn't mean—"

"Don't do it again."

They're gone and a faint perfume lingers in the air: a smell of limes and lemons with a touch of *flores* . . .

And I'm strolling home, stripping leaves off the trees overhead. That didn't last, either, I think. Nothing seems to last. Maybe I should get myself another dog: a big German shepherd to follow me around and keep people at bay.

Or a cat: yeah, I'll get myself a Siamese cat. That will be my trademark. People will nudge each other and say, *Hey, here comes Clint the Cat!* And I'll swagger into public places, lithe and cool, that cat draped around my neck like a collar . . .

The stars hold me there in our front yard for a while. Then I go upstairs and work on Moon City for an hour. There's no reason I can't win that prize.

I haven't even mentioned it to Mom and Dad. If no one knows you *want* to win, how can you disappoint them?

21

The last thing I pack for the camping trip is the pistol. (That was the first mistake I made.) I've bought shells and I think maybe we'll have some good target practice. Then, holding the gun, I know better: that's not why I'm taking it.

Four A.M. is earlier than dinosaurs, but I'm ready when Bud arrives. We throw my stuff into the trunk, then we're on the road in his dad's Plymouth. I think of Ellie as we zip through Southtown: brother or not, I'm going to call her when we get back.

But for now it's all behind us, the whole crazy world: school and rules and home and rules and people and stupid remarks; neon signs and pictures in my head—and shadows hanging around darkened stadiums. I'm about to tell Bud about that when he yells:

"Yip-peee."

"Yip-peeeeeee," I yell.

The sky is the color of plums and by six we're sitting in a truck stop, plugging the jukebox and watching the sun come up.

"You know what?" I tell Bud. "When school's out I may hitchhike to the West Coast. Might even get a pad on the beach. Who knows? I might end up in the movies."

"Your middle name is *might*."

Outside there's a whole armada of trucks. When the waitress arrives, she gives us a long look.

"You guys don't drive a truck, do you?"

"Sure," I say. "We're on our way to California."

"You're awful young," she says. "Which truck is yours?"

Bud picks out a huge, silver-blue rig and points:

"It's that big Mack," he says.

"Hmm," she says. "Didn't know you could drive a hamburger."

22

Just after nine we're heading into the mountains. We call them mountains, though I guess they're big hills. Green and blue with cliffs of granite, they swell toward the horizon. Nestled within them there's a small lake that's hard to find in the wilderness area. Bud and I know an old logging road that's not even on the map. We turn off the main highway and find our private road.

It hasn't been used since the last snowfall, and I jump out and move branches and fallen tree limbs. Then we bump and bounce and weave through the trees until we see the lake: jade green and isolated, it's still as glass and there's not a soul in sight.

The trees are thick and hushed and evergreens make the air spicy. We're unpacking the car and I show Bud the gun wrapped in paper.

"What'd you bring that for?"

"Target practice—in case we get bored."

"Oh, man, why don't you throw it away?"

"It's a good one. Besides, I bought shells. You gun-shy?"

"Maybe. I just don't like those things."

I walk back toward the rear of the car. Even in all that gorgeous privacy, there's a chill of fear. Of what I'm not sure. Only that *things aren't what they used to be*.

"Come on," Bud yells. "Let's go swimmin'."

But I don't move. Things are not the same because I am not the same. And it is still there, the picture, flickering inside my head, and I don't want to see it. I wrap the pistol back up and stick it in the car trunk.

That was the second big mistake I made.

23

In the early afternoon, Bud finds me propped against a tree with a pad and a pen.

"What're you doin'?" he says.

"Workin' on the science project."

"Man, you need a vacation."

"The deadline's just a few days away."

"You'll make it. Come on. Let's go fishin'."

In tin plates I dish up steaming piles of fried potatoes and onions and golden slabs of fresh catfish rolled in corn meal and fried crispy brown.

"Oh, man," Bud says, "this is livin'."

For the first time in weeks I don't have a single unpleasant thought in my head. We lounge around the campfire, and the owl hoots and the random calls of nightbirds are the most beautiful sounds in the world.

It's been a great day. We've seen a deer, a fox, and two beavers. I don't ever want to go back.

(Back to TV rumors about bombings and wars and other disasters. Back to the familiar trap of city streets where, more often that not, I'm running with a crazy, half-formed picture in my mind. Back to places where shadows move . . .)

I tell Bud about what happened in the stadium.

"Have you mentioned it to the coach?"

"No."

"Hall, you're somethin'. Why don't you *tell* people things."

It's quiet again. A fox calls through the stilled trees. Something splashes in the lake.

"People used to live like this all the time," I say. "They were freer. They must have been."

I'm remembering old Dub that night in jail. I can almost hear his voice . . .

. . . We've lost contact with nature. Not only the real world of grass and trees and lakes and streams, but our *nature. We've lost touch with ourselves and each other. We stopped sharing; stopped telling each other what it's really like . . .*

So when we climb into the tent, I think: I'll level with Bud. I'll tell him how it is with me. We lie there, bathed in the priceless air, taking in the silence. Both ends of the tent are opened and through one flap the blue velvet sky is thick with diamond stars.

Already I've forgotten the reality of Jory Hall, a.k.a. Clint the Cat and Jory the Great. I'm drifting up through the myriad stars, practicing my speech as President of the Universe.

Bud says: "Did you know Cara's dad died? Cirrhosis of the liver?"

"Why'd you have to bring that up?"

"It's—reality."

"That's what we came up here to get away from—stuff like that."

So Bud's quiet but he's got me thinking about all the stuff inside me that nobody knows.

". . . Bud . . . Did you ever find yourself—actually hating someone you were supposed to love?"

"I don't think so. Why?"

"Oh . . . Just somethin' I saw on TV . . ."

24

After a long day's hike deep into the hills, we return to camp. We shuck our backpacks and clothes and swim for a while like dolphins. Huge clouds, the size of battleships, line up in the west above the hilltops.

"Think it'll rain?" Bud says.

"No. We're too lucky."

But it does—suddenly: Pouring in buckets, it splashes us good while we're eating. We grab our food and rush for the tent, but we haven't ditched it and water runs in.

The rain shows no sign of letting up and we decide we'd better navigate the old road while we still can. The car slips and slides and twice I have to get out and push. The rain feels great on my back and I'm barefoot and there's mud up to my knees, and I love it. We get to the improved road and Bud says:

"Which way?"

"Left."

We wind and wind around for what seems an hour. We're both still sopping wet, and the rain's still falling in thick sheets. Up ahead there's a place to park where people stop for the view. We pull into it.

I fiddle around with the radio, and Bud says we ought to think about the battery; we might be there a long time. So I settle back, watching the silver-gray splashes on the windshield.

And I'm thinking: Jory, it's stupid to stay so locked up all the time. You're making yourself sick over something that's not all that big. Besides, show some spirit. The least you can do is *talk* to somebody.

"Bud . . ."

"Yeah?"

"Man, there's somethin' I want to tell you."

"Go ahead. Shoot."

"It's been on my mind for a long time . . . It's about Reve . . ."

(There *is* such a thing as fate—or accident. Bad timing, that's another word for it. I'd just said a few words about that night, standing outside Reve's room in the hall . . . There's a funny sound outside the car.)

"What's that?" I say.

"Sounded like a car door slamming."

I lean toward the glass on my side and peer into the rain. It takes a few seconds to realize that I'm looking into a pair of eyes.

"What the—"

I slam my fist down on the door lock just as someone tries the door handle.

"What is it?" Bud says.

"Lock your door," I say.

Bud reaches for the lock and this guy jerks the door open. So there's at least two of them, I think. This guy stands there in an olive drab raincoat staring at us.

The other one joins him—a big man. He looks kind of like Rod Steiger with a mustache.

"Lemme see your driver's license," the big man says.

"Who are you, anyway?" I ask.

"Smokey the Bear."

It turns out he's the sheriff and a deputy is with him. They're looking for some guys who robbed a service station. The deputy takes the keys and starts rummaging through the trunk.

"Look, Sheriff," I say. "We're just on a trip. We've been camping down by the lake."

"Why'd you leave?"

"The rain."

"You mean your tent's not waterproof?"

"It was the old logging road. We were afraid we'd get stuck and couldn't get out."

He hands Bud his driver's license, and I'm convinced he believes us. Then the deputy walks up with a big smile. Dangling from two fingers is the pistol.

25

"I'm sorry, man," I tell Bud. "If it hadn't been for the gun . . ."

Bud says nothing. We're in a small room just off the sheriff's office. He's been on the phone a long time. I wonder who he's talking to.

There's not much in the room: a beat-up old desk, an antique typewriter, and three metal folding chairs. On one wall are three stuffed heads: a bear, a fox, a deer. The gleaming deer's eyes remind me of Ellie.

"Gross," I say.

"What?"

"Putting heads up like that."

"As long as they're not ours . . ."

Tweaking his mustache, the sheriff fills the doorway.

"You," he says, pointing at me. "You look like a thinker. Come in here."

Thoughtless, I follow him into the other room, and he doesn't offer a chair or anything. From a nest of papers, he picks up a pad.

"You Bud?"

"I'm Jory."

"OK, Jory. I checked out you boys' drivers' licenses. And the car's OK and neither of you have a record. There's just one little matter . . ."

Holding the pistol, as though it might be a live snake, he waves it back and forth.

"This is pretty serious, you know that?"

"I—I found it."

"Oh?"

"In an alley."

"An alley beside the lake, huh?"

"I brought it with me—from Marshal. That's where I found it."

"Why'd you bring it with you?"

"I thought—some target practice might be fun."

"Any particular target?"

"No. You know . . ."

"You found the shells, too, I guess?"

"No, I bought 'em."

"For target practice?"

"Yes."

". . . What were you doing in the alley where you found the gun?"

"Running."

"From what?"

"Just—running. I run all over town. I was taking a shortcut."

". . . Well, young man, you'd better be telling me the truth. Wait here . . ."

Waddling like a bear, he disappears into the room with Bud. He's gone for a long time, and I'm getting sick. The trip was the highlight of the year, and I've messed it up. When the sheriff returns, Bud is following, staring at the floor.

The sheriff says: "Tell you what, boys. Gonna give you a break. Gonna let you go—on one condition . . . I talked with both your dads. And if you're not home in about five hours, you'll have to settle with me—and a formal charge."

"But we've got another whole day left," I say.

"Not up here, you don't. You're expected at home—soon as you can make the drive."

We walk out to the car and Bud is stiff and cold as icicles. I try to talk to him. Pure Iceburger.

26

"Bud?"

He won't say a word or give a single sign that I'm in the car. We're moving too fast, too, but I'm afraid to mention that.

"Come on, Bud. Say something."

"All right. Why'd you have to bring that gun?"

"I just thought—"

"I don't think you think at all. You ruined the entire trip."

There's not much to say, so I count telephone poles until I get mixed up.

"Bud . . . The Science Prize pays a hundred dollars. We'll use it for another trip."

"The *Science* Prize? You haven't even won it yet. You know somethin' else? You live in a dream world, Hall."

"No, I don't."

"You do. You're always talkin' about what you're *going* to do."

"What's wrong with making plans?"

"They're always *your* plans. You never think of anyone but yourself."

"Come on, Bud. We're good friends. Let's don't—"

"Friends? How can anyone be friends with you? You never tell anybody anything—'cept some big idea."

Beside the road, construction workers are digging a large hole. I wish I was in it.

". . . I'm sorry, Bud."

"Save it."

At home Bud waits just long enough for me to get my stuff out of the trunk. Then, spinning his wheels, he speeds off without a word.

As expected, Dad is waiting up. I avoid him by going past him to the kitchen. But he follows.

"Why a gun, Jory, of all things?"

I'm tired and I really can't explain. I don't know how to tell him that things have changed—nothing seems the same—and I'm just barely in control. I don't know how to tell him I'm a failure and that I'd like to make up for it.

"I just—found it," I say. "It was wrong to keep it. Wrong to buy the shells. Color me wrong."

Now my voice is getting all funny. I don't even recognize myself.

"Jory, is it all just one big joke to you?"

"No . . . You ought to know me better than that. Don't you?"

"Yes. You're right . . . It's late. Go on to bed . . . Sleep well."

It was more than just disappointing Bud or my parents—more than another run-in with the law. It was the beginning of the end of a kind of innocence: the idea that I would change—if I only changed my surroundings. But a gun is a gun in an alley or by a tree-lined lake. The same goes for a confused, out-of-breath high-school senior.

So the world grew smaller after our trip. Smaller, less distinct, more shadowy. Perhaps its—the world's—craziness grew more obvious, for I tried harder to avoid it.

27

The sun's up high when I wake up. It's a bright, clear, warm, spring, young, good, May day. But I give it a D minus. I think maybe I'll stay in bed: there I'll have no friends to lose, no girls to keep out too late . . . And no shadows in my mind, or in an empty stadium.

And I'm thinking: Everything's moving too fast—things just keep happening and happening and I can't keep up with them. It's like trying to run a race with the best long-distance runner in the country—and my legs are too short.

Like trying to run a race with Reve, and not wanting to at the same time . . .

Hunger pulls me out of bed, into my clothes and down the stairs. Tiger Jory, the hungry beast, prowls around downstairs. No one's there, but my place is set at the table. There's juice and a bowl of raisin bran and beside it a note:

Young Jory,
Keep laughing. Practice for life.
            Love,
            Mom

I'm almost finished eating when I see her through the window. She's in the backyard in a lounge chair. She's been reading but the book is in her lap and she's leaning her head back and there's an expression on her face I've never seen.

Briefly, she's a different person: older somehow, wistful, and there's a kind of hurt, too. And I think: I've done that. I've hurt the last person in the world I'd want to hurt. I can't *keep* from hurting people.

I go out back and she smiles and I pick up a stick and that doesn't help, so I pick up a rock and hit a tree with it. I am so talented I can't believe myself.

"Mom . . ."

"Yes."

"I'm going to get a job. I talked with Mr. Meyers at his men's store a few months ago. He said come in toward the end of school. I'll go see him."

"Good. I think you'd enjoy working in a men's store."

"Why?"

"You're neat and you wear clothes well."

"I do?"

"Yes. And you have a good sense of color."

"Reve's the one with color. He could wear clothes that stopped traffic."

"Reve is—special. But you're special, too, Jory. You must remember that."

"How am I special?"

"For one thing you draw like da Vinci himself. And you're one of the most spontaneous people I've ever known. That's a very refreshing quality—a delightful quality."

". . . Mom, I don't like to get in trouble. I don't *feel* like a troublemaker."

"I know."

"That pistol was just—stupid. It was there—in the trunk of the car. We didn't even fire it."

"I believe you."

"You do?"

"Yes. I don't think you'd lie to me. And I hope you know you never have to."

". . . Is there—anything I can do for you—anything at all?"

"Laugh a little more," she says.

28

Mr. Meyers who owns the Band Box men's store is neither old nor young. Like my dad he's at the in-between age, but the difference is that Mr. Meyers almost never stops talking. His office is full of new clothes he's inspecting, and the desk is cluttered with samples of men's cologne he's thinking of buying. I'm trying to get a word or two in edgewise.

"I can start Monday," I say. "I've got a good sense of color and—"

"Here," he says, a bottle of cologne in hand. "Try this one. It's called Lark."

"I don't wear that stuff, Mr. Meyers."

"Just try a little on your arm there."

So he dabs some on my arm and waves the bottle under his nose.

"Kind of a dark smell," he says. "Should be called Mudlark . . . Try this—Midnight Hours. Sounds like an old B movie."

He keeps dabbing me with the stuff—Kayak and Panther and Deep Woods, names like that.

"No, no, no," he says. "That won't do. That's so deep

in the woods you'd never get out. People would take one whiff and just leave you there . . . Let's try Prowl . . ."

I'm getting dizzy from all those aromas and I try to tell him a few more things and he interrupts.

"I know you'd be good, Jory. You're Reve's brother. Reve bought all his clothes here . . . Now, let's see. Here's an interesting bottle. It's called Everglades."

So I get up. I'm tired of being a guinea pig and I'm tired of being Reve Hall's brother.

"OK," he says. "Be here at nine o'clock Monday morning."

Then I'm on the street feeling like a million dollars, but I'm smelling like a thousand flowers and bushels of citrus fruit. I imagine that guys are stopping to point and girls are turning to stare.

And I'm imagining that traffic has come to a halt: people are getting out of their cars to see what this cloud of scent is all about. Now planes are circling, trying to land, to check out this new aroma.

The WPIX helicopter is hovering overhead, filming me with its TV camera.

And in New York, they mention me on the CBS Evening News.

I practically fly home to tell Dad the good news. He's out back putting gas in the lawnmower. After I tell him, I keep waiting. Not even a weak smile crosses his face.

"That's fine," he says finally. "That's just fine, but—"

"But?"

"I've already got you a job, Jory."

"*You* got me one? Where?"

"The Rexall Drug. I spoke with Freda Norris this morning."

My mind's a computer: That's the place where Reve used to work—that's one thing. But the main thing is that he's figured out a way to keep his eye on me. Freda Norris will act as jailer and number one informer. Besides, who wants to be up to his elbows in ice cream all day?

"Dad, it's all set. I'm supposed to start Monday."

"You'll just have to call Mr. Meyers. Freda is expecting you."

"Whether I like it or not, huh?"

"It's best, Jory. You've not done so well lately—managing your life. Give this a try."

Guilty people give up easily. Guilty people are already beaten so it doesn't take much to make them tame as eggs.

I shrug.

"OK, Dad. Whatever you say."

I work all afternoon on Moon City. At least *it's* coming along well. Houses and apartments rise in tiers beneath the domes, kind of like the Habitat at the Montreal World's Fair. And everywhere there are miniparks and fountains.

There's a huge stack of drawings on my desk. I'll show them, I'm thinking. I'll show everybody . . .

29

I didn't know, until much later, how much the Science Prize meant to me. It would, in my mind, make up for everything else.

The week before graduation I worked every night until 3 A.M. My right arm ached from gripping a pen. Page by page the project grew and my confidence with it.

Until thirty minutes before the deadline, I perfected the drawings and the ideas behind them. When I presented a huge folder to the principal, he couldn't believe it.

"Forty *pages?* This must really mean a lot to you, Jory."

"Aw," I said. "Just somethin' to do . . ."

Then it's graduation night. The whole day has been like a Sunday, and I can't believe the school year is over.

In the auditorium, after we've marched in and the orchestra's still playing, I'm wondering: Is graduation the beginning of something new—good—or just the end of something hard to understand? . . . I can't decide.

The guest speaker is telling us about our bright and glorious futures. I'm thinking about the hundred bucks that goes with the Science Prize. Maybe I *won't* spend it on a camping trip. Who needs Bud Mavis, anyway?

Who needs a guy who likes burritos with mayonnaise, for gosh sakes? Or a guy with a baby face you could make from a package of Jello pudding? Who needs a guy who's as colorful as a fog light, with as many ideas as a box of Cracker Jacks?

Maybe I'll make a down payment on a car—a blue Trans Am with a white racing stripe and—

They're handing out the awards, and I sit up. The winners will be on TV and in all the papers. What's more important, I'll have something to put on my wall—some *proof* that I ever went to high school at all.

Ellie's sitting a few seats down the row and she leans forward and raises her crossed fingers. I smile.

. . . And I get out of the spaceship where I'm greeted by dignitaries, and the new citizens of Moon City break into waves of applause. I climb to a special platform, and a hush settles over the crowd. I pull the switch.

The domes of the city of the future are ablaze with light: gold and silver, pale copper and deep bronze. A new age is underway; a new era for mankind . . .

"And now for the Science Prize," says the principal.

I grip the arms of the seat and make my face go blank in case anyone's looking. He's telling everyone how important the prize is and how the competition this year was especially keen. There's a long pause. I close my eyes.

". . . goes to Durbin Raynard."

And I watch him muscle his way toward the stage—like Reve, I'm thinking; he looks like Reve—and I can't quite believe it. Durbin designed a car—just a *car* that would run on batteries—and I designed a whole city.

But he's up there, grinning like an ape, and there are flashbulbs popping—he'll be on the late news. What makes it worse, he's one of the jocks I tangled with that night—the one I pushed against the Camaro . . .

The reception for the seniors is noisy and crowded and I don't want to be there. But I stay for Mom and Dad, and when I see the principal, I corner him.

"Oh, Jory. Congratulations."

"For what?"

"Well—graduating. Believe me, Jory, the decision for the prize was a tough one."

"Could you tell me what—what made you decide?"

"Well—practicality, I think. Probability. You see, a car like Durbin's is something we need—today. It's an idea that can sell, Jory, and help Durbin sell himself."

"Who's going to buy him?"

"What's that?"

"I was just wondering . . . What's more practical than tomorrow? Someone's got to plan for it."

"True. True. But to quote a famous writer: 'It is in the here and now that we must live.' "

Before I go, I get all my drawings.

I'll show them, I think: I'll show them all. I'll sell my plans to NASA. I'll get an all-expense-paid trip to Houston.

We leave by a side door, my big idea tucked under my arm like a kid nobody wants.

Now I'm sure someone will hire Durbin Raynard. He'll go to work in Detroit. He'll come up with a new line of cars called Shark, Squid, and Octopus. Finally he'll win a big prize for the ultimate car—a car that eats other cars—an XL Piranha Fish.

30

"I think you can do something with your idea," Ellie says. "I really do."

"Yeah. Paper my wall."

The Good Buddy Drive-In sign flashes on and off, reflected in the hood of the car. I've taken Ellie there instead of Winslow's where the crowd will be.

"Jory, don't talk like that. Can I see it sometime, the whole thing?"

"Yeah, I guess. It's not exactly in demand."

I change the subject and we start talking about what we're going to do this summer. She'll be helping her mother clean peoples' houses. I think that's an awful job to look forward to, but mine's not exactly glamorous.

"In the fall," Ellie says, "maybe I can go to college. You're going, aren't you?"

"I don't know . . . Mom keeps asking me. I can't make up my mind."

And I'm thinking: Young Jory, what *is* it you want, anyway?

(I didn't know the answer then, because I thought that

some *thing* would satisfy me. But what I wanted was just to feel right inside. Just that.)

When I pull away from the drive-in, I give the car too much gas and the tires squeal. I drive clear out to Deer Creek and park beside it. We've got the windows down and you can hear the water running and crickets chirping and frogs making frog sounds.

"I wish we lived out here," Ellie says.

I'm not sure whether she means her family or the two of us, but I say:

"Me, too."

"Jory . . . You ever think about—getting married?"

"No. Do you?"

"Sometimes . . . I just—I want to get away from home. That's an awful thing to say, but—it's so crowded there. And there's never any privacy . . . Oh, well, I shouldn't talk about it."

"It's OK to talk about it."

"You never talk about things like that—personal things. Doesn't anything ever bother you?"

"I guess I'm easygoing."

And I say to myself: You're an easygoing liar, too.

"I think you take things seriously," Ellie says.

"Some things."

"You're an interesting combination. Part daredevil and—thinker."

"I think too much."

"About what?"

"Oh—my brother. See, Reve could do anything. He was an athlete and a scholar and—everything. Me, I— "

"You can't compare yourself with him, Jory. He's a different person."

I feel it building then, just bubbling up inside me. And I know if I don't get it out, it will just go on and on getting worse.

"Ellie, I—I—One night, I—"

"What is it, Jory?"

" . . . Nothin'."

"It must be *something*. You were all excited."

I turn the radio on and keep it low. It's slow dance music and I remember how well she can dance. She's settled back against the car seat, looking all soft.

"Jory . . . Did you ever feel so—lonesome you could hug a tree?"

"Sometimes . . ."

After the longest pause in history, I slide across the seat toward her. She doesn't move a bit; just closes her eyes. I put my arm around her and I kiss her. She puts her hand on my arm and kind of grips me, and I kiss her again. Her lips are very soft, and I kiss her once more and then I feel funny.

I'm thinking: What am I doing, anyway? Ellie Huerta's a Chicano and she's fat. No one would take her out but me. Then I'm hating myself for thinking that. I really am.

"It's getting late," I say. "We'd better go."

Driving back it keeps building inside; pictures flash inside my head. When I get home, I hear a siren a few blocks away. It's like it's part of me, sending out a warning.

31

The Moon City project is sitting on my desk where I left it. I open the orange cover and then I slam it shut. And I'm outside in the hall, walking around before I even realize what I'm doing. The door to Reve's room is open.

I flip on the light and collapse on his bed. There's the big, stuffed bear he won at a school carnival. And in a neat glass frame on the wall is the award for being the Outstanding Senior.

I've got a little paperweight in my hands that I picked up from his desk. I'm turning it over and over in my hands, staring at the framed award.

I don't even remember throwing the paperweight. It hits the glass and it shatters all over the floor. I'm staring at the pieces when Dad rushes in.

"What happened?"

"I—I broke some glass."

"Jory, what *is* it?"

Mom comes to the door and Dad goes over to her.

"Let me handle this, Linda. Please. Go back to bed."

She disappears and I'm picking up the glass.

"Leave that, Jory."

Dad closes the door, and I'm still picking up glass.

"I said *leave* it . . . Now sit down—please."

So I fold up in the chair at Reve's desk. I pick at the hem of my jeans and Dad adjusts his glasses.

"I want to know what's going on," he says.

"I don't know."

"Well, I think you *do* know . . . Are you upset because of the Science Prize?"

"I guess I wanted to win."

"We can't win all the time."

"How can you lose all the time?"

"You did the best you could. And you know your mother and I are proud of you, don't you?"

"For what? I can't do anything right."

"That's not true, but I understand the feeling, so let's deal with that . . . You know—seventeen is not very old. You haven't been on this earth very long, Jory. You're not very far away from childhood. Everything's still new. And you're at the age that . . . Is it a girl that's bothering you?"

"No."

"Reve had girl problems. Everyone thought he was happy-go-lucky all the time. But Reve—"

"It's nothing like that."

". . . Did you break that glass on purpose?"

"Yes. Well, I—just did it."

"Then you must have been angry at something—or someone . . . You know, Reve was under lots of pressure, too, Jory. Oh, he didn't show it much, but he really was. When you start winning, people keep expecting you to win and—"

I'm up, striding across the floor.

"Reve," I say. "It's always Reve. Reve this and Reve that."

"That's not true."

"What am I supposed to do? I'm not an athlete like he was. I'm not—"

"No one expects you to be."

"Then why all the talk? Coach brags about him. Mr. Willard raves about him, and you're *always* talking about him."

"Are you *angry* at Reve?"

"I just—I'm like a carbon copy or something. I can't even be myself."

"Jory, that's in *your* mind."

"Then why'd you get me the job he used to have? I could get my own job. I did, didn't I?"

"Freda was looking for someone she could really count on. I mentioned you because you're very self-reliant, Jory, and you're—"

"You did it so she could spy on me. You did it 'cause Reve used to work there and—"

"No!"

Dad's up now. He's kind of flushed and he jerks his glasses off.

"Now, Jory, I want you to sit down."

"I'm tired. I—"

"Sit *down!*"

I sit.

". . . You've blown this all out of proportion. No one—especially your mother and I—ever expected you to be like Reve. First of all, you seem to think Reve never had any problems. I could tell you—well, never mind. The thing is, there's something not right in *your* mind about Reve, isn't that true?"

". . . I guess."

"Don't just guess, Jory. What is it—a grudge? Do you resent him?"

"I—I guess I wanted to be like him and I couldn't. I can't do much of anything."

"Feeling sorry for yourself won't help. Besides, you are different. You think Reve could've designed that city? Or me or your mother, for that matter?"

"A lot of good it did me."

"That attitude again. Jory, with that attitude, you're

. . . Oh, well . . . Look, whatever's between you and
Reve, I want you to get it straight. Would it help to talk
to a psychiatrist?"

"You think I'm crazy?"

"No. Sometimes talking to a professional helps."

"I'll work it out."

"I hope so . . . And Jory, I'll always be here if you
want to talk. Always. OK?"

"OK."

I go down to my room and there's a sandwich and
milk and a piece of cake on a tray. And there's a note from
Mom.

Young Jory,
Thought you might be hungry.
Keep practicing. It gets easier . . .
Love,
Mother

When the lights are out, I'm very still, as though I'm afraid
to move. It's like being on the edge of something without
an edge. The picture keeps flickering inside my head. I
toss and turn, but it won't go away.

It's Reve. It's been Reve all the time . . . *standing in*
his room in front of the mirror, flexing his muscles. He looks
like Adonis or someone. I'm watching him from the hallway. And
then I'm thinking: I wish he had a big scar on his back. I wish
he'd hurt himself. I wish—

Rolling over I press my face into the pillow until I think
I'm going to suffocate. The picture fades out. Still, I can't
sleep.

I slip out of the house and stand in the backyard.
There's a faint weird sound and I try to ignore it. Finally
I hunt through the dark and there's a tiny bird. It's fallen
from its nest, and it's hurt. I stare and stare and then my
eyes are all watery and I slam my foot down on it.

It makes me kind of sick, but I scoop it up in a can

and carry it out to my private graveyard. I put it in a small hole.

I'm kneeling there in the moonlight. I don't want to be the way I am. The moon's like a blue light gone crazy. And I've got the only dead zoo in the world.

PART TWO
THE YOUNG MAN

1

In most so-called primitive societies, I've read, there are certain rituals for adolescents. These trials or feats mark the young male's passage from boy to man.

We don't have that in Western cultures. In America, we have war and we have football. If you are lucky—or unlucky—enough to miss both, what do you do? How do you prove yourself? . . .

The stadium is overwarm, shadowy, almost eerie—a whale's skeleton through which I run. Dog days of summer they call it: long, enervating days, drawn out like bad movies.

Outrun the summer, Jory! Break the time barrier . . . I do twenty laps. I'm preparing for the Autumn Olympics by working in a drugstore all day. I'm turning into an exotic vegetable: a cross between a squash and an asparagus—a squaragus.

I take a rest on the bleachers to get my breath. I'm not even thinking of the shadow up there when it—he—appears, stealthily at first, from a lower ramp. I can't believe it. It's Coach Pelham.

"Jory?"

Coach Pelham? All those nights up there—watching me?

"How's it goin'?" I say.

"Fine . . . Been watching you. You've really got speed."

"How come?"

"What?"

"Why've you been watching me all this time?"

"Just a few minutes. I just got here. Been checking out football equipment."

"You haven't watched me before?"

"That once—the night we talked. Why?"

". . . Nothin'."

"Mind if I sit?"

"No."

"Nice night."

"Hot as old ladies' Buicks."

"Yeah . . . You enrolled in college yet?"

"No."

"Why?"

"I don't know."

"I'd encourage you to. I've even spoken about you to Fred Larmee. He's track coach at the university."

"Why'd you mention me?"

"You've got something, Jory."

"Heartburn."

"A sense of humor among other things . . . You know—I think about guys like you a lot—the ones that weren't on the teams. The thing is, Jory, at your age, you need to zero in on that special thing—and develop it."

"I tried."

"The Science Prize?"

"I'll win the Nobel next year."

". . . I'm going to level with you. I saw your entry and I think you should have won. I told the board that, too."

"Why?"

"Because—Jory, what is this with you, anyway?"

"What?"

"Acting like you're a leper . . . You're a *very* likable guy."

"They want me for the cover of *Boy's Life*."

"You . . . You're not Reve, Jory."

"Who said I was?"

"Your eyes."

Of all the things I'd heard at school, that was the strangest—especially coming from Coach Pelham. I blink a couple of times in the moonlight. I study my shoes. Jory the Great: The Marathon Kid.

". . . I'm afraid I owe you another apology, Jory. That afternoon in the locker room . . . I was already upset when I got there. I'm sorry I made such a thing out of it."

"That's OK."

"I've done a lot of thinking, Jory. This will be my last year of coaching. There's—something wrong with this— team system—this tiresome emphasis on winning games and trophies . . . You guys—kids like yourself—miss out. You need . . . Did you know that for years—centuries maybe—the object of athletics was to bring glory and honor to the human body? And to That which created it?"

"I guess I read that somewhere."

"All that's been lost, and it's too bad. It's—beautiful, the human body, and especially at your age."

"I—I never thought about it."

"You're more unusual than I thought—never to think about the body."

"I—well—you just—everybody has one . . ."

"Jory, you—I've noticed a certain shyness about you— in the locker room, even in PT class. Is it anything—you know—you might want to talk about?"

"I—well . . . Who likes to play grab-ass in the shower? It's dumb."

"Yes, it is. Like lots of things—drugs and booze and fighting and war . . ."

"Then why do we have all that stuff? Everybody *knows* it's dumb."

"In a word—insanity: the inability to profit from past mistakes."

(For one brief moment that summer—before the sky dissolved and the moon became a hospital—I was no longer a mere solo. There arose in the gloom of that stadium a fragile duet, a boy-man song, and as quickly it would fade.)

"I better be going," I say, getting up.

"Jory . . . Don't ever stop trying. And—especially—don't stop caring."

"For what?"

"Something. Anything . . . Seems to me anybody who can come up with an idea like yours is *capable* of caring for just about everything."

". . . Coach?"

"Yeah."

"I'm sorry, too—'bout that day in the locker room. My attitude was bad. I was wrong."

"Welcome to the human race, Jory."

For a while I thought I'd been initiated into that mysterious world of adulthood. For a brief while all shadow vanished. But only for a while . . .

2

My boss, Freda Norris, is an efficiency expert, and I've decided women are like that when they're by themselves. (Mom's that way at home—always cleaning whether anything's dirty or not.)

Freda is never still: She marches around the drugstore all day with a big clipboard. She's always checking the shelves to see if we need anything—and to see if I've marked the right prices. Today she comes up to the fountain where I've just handed this girl a double-dip ice-cream cone.

"Jory, you must remember we're here to make a profit. P-r-o-f-i-t. When you scoop up the ice cream, be sure the scoop is only level full. L-e-v-e-l. Without lots of ice cream hanging around the edges. Any questions?"

"N-o-n-e," I say.

The weeks go by. I don't even have time for a tan. If I get any paler I'll be a mushroom and some real Crazy will use me in a recipe—a big surprise dish: a Taco Oh-Oh.

I swallow my pride and call Bud's house. His mother says he's got a job out of town. Who needs him, anyway?

I think. But I'm kind of excited when I get a card in his own inimitable handwriting—part English, part Chinese:

Hey, man, what's happening? You ought to be here. I'm a bronze god, and the chicks are outasight. Gained ten pounds—all muscle. How's Ellie? See you in September.

Bud

What's happening is I'm in a drugstore—a *soda* jerk—and the whole world's getting bronze as a statue, healthy as trees outside. Bud's got a job on a farm upstate and what have I got? A dead zoo in the backyard.

And something else, too. I rarely admit it to myself, but it's there, the fear. It's not large and it's not *too* noticeable—kind of like a hum that I'm barely aware of in the background.

There's this idea growing, too, that nothing is quite what I thought it was. And because no single thing is predictable, then *anything* might happen at any time . . .

3

At home I begin to notice things. One day it's just an old house on a street with lots of trees. Then it's like I haven't really looked at it: it really *is* old and needs painting in places and its rooms whisper half-known things.

And our furniture. It's not beat up or anything, but you can see the worn spots when the sun shines on it. I used to wonder why we didn't have a new house further out like most kids my age. Now I wonder if we live here because we *have* to.

Then there's all the medical books my dad reads. They're always piled around his big chair and on his bed-side table. One night I ask him:

"How come you read those books all the time?"

"Oh—they help in my profession."

"But you're a salesman."

"Well, pharmaceuticals and medicine, you know, they're kind of a pair. And to tell the truth I once wanted to be a doctor."

"I didn't know that."

"Quite a few years ago."

"What changed your mind?"

"Reve first. Then you. You get a family, Jory, things—change."

I'm uncomfortable, as though he's about to say something I don't want to hear. I go on upstairs and change into running clothes. When I come down he's still reading.

"You like being a salesman, Dad?"

"It's—all right."

I kind of grin, then I'm out in the fresh air, running down the street, and everything's fine. They keep the stadium gate locked in summer, but I climb over the steel fence and start around the track.

Five laps. Six. Seven, and I'm not even winded. I could go the distance, I think—I really could. A marathon runner. But after twelve laps I collapse on the bottom row of the bleachers. And way up high there's a slight movement.

I'm real cool, like I don't see anything. Whistling, I'm up strolling along, swinging my arms. But my heart is pounding. *He's right up there—right above me!* Then I charge straight up the steps.

Whoever it is runs toward a ramp. It's a man, not much larger than myself. At the ramp opening, I stop, listening to running steps on the concrete.

"What do you want?" I yell. "Who *are* you? What do you *want?*"

My voice echoes down the empty ramp.

I'm sweating, about to collapse, when I get home. I'm in the front yard, scanning the street, as though the shadow's still there. Dad comes around the block, strolling toward the house.

"Been for a walk," he says.

Then he's staring at me, and it seems like he's doing lots of that these days. Staring. Like I'm *crazy.* And I'm thinking: *Am* I? . . . AM I?

And I feel worse when I realize I don't know who I'm asking.

4

Usually I'm hip to what's playing at the drive-in. But it's getting so I'm preoccupied all the time. I just hand the guy the money and drive on in, holding Ellie's hand.

We're sitting close and I can't believe the movie. There's a sniper in this stadium during a big bowl game. He's going to waste a bunch of people.

"I'll be back," I say.

I climb out of the car. I kind of trot toward the snack bar; then I'm running. I'm swigging a Coke when Ellie comes in.

"You OK?"

"Yeah. Just—my stomach."

"Was it the movie?"

"Naw, I—"

"I didn't like it either . . . Jory, you're not in trouble or anything, are you?"

"No. Why?"

"You're uptight, kinda."

"I told you. My stomach is—"

"It's not just tonight . . ."

We wait until the dumb show is over and then we go

back to the car. With the sound turned off, it's nice and private.

"Jory . . . I saw the cutest little apartment today—just right for two people. It was only a hundred dollars a month. Even couples our age could afford that."

"I guess . . . Say, you want some popcorn?"

"No, thanks . . . If a man works and the woman works, too, you could really save some money."

I'm fiddling with the radio and the dumb knob comes off in my hand.

"Jory, I think—if something doesn't happen, I'll—I'll run away from home."

"Aw, heck, Ellie, where would you go?"

"Plains City maybe."

"What would you do there?"

"I don't know. Wouldn't make much difference . . . Would you care if I left?"

"Sure."

"I doubt it. Nobody cares much."

"Yes, they do."

"Jory, I can't stand it at home. And I hate my job and—"

I'm afraid she's going to cry, but she just sighs.

"Que lástima."

"What's that mean?"

"What a pity . . . Poor Elena."

"It won't last forever, you know."

"What?"

"The job. Being at home."

"It *is* forever, every day . . . Jory, just drop me somewhere. I'm a mess."

"I'm a mess, too. Hi, mess."

"You know something? I really don't care anymore."

"About what?"

"Anything . . ."

The second movie is a comedy, and we relax a little. When it's over, it's late and I drive her home.

"Have you ever been—desperate, Jory?"

"Yeah. I think."

"When you are," she says, "you'll know."

Driving home, I think: Why am I going out with her, anyway? . . . But I know. I like her a lot. She's the one sure thing in my life: one thing—unchanging, unthreatening—for me. And I don't want to do anything to hurt her. Nothing. She's been hurt enough.

It did not even faintly occur to me that it is difficult enough to protect one's self, let alone another person. And I had not counted in any way on Reve's coming home . . .

5

Freda Norris listens to my bright idea. She's got a big ear for p-r-o-f-i-t.

". . . Health drinks," I say. "I'll use high-protein powder and raw eggs, and maybe brewer's yeast, lots of fresh fruit and ice cream. There's nothing like it in town."

I'm surprised when she says OK. I go out and buy the stuff and spend the afternoon making signs for the window. Freda likes the names I've made up for special drinks: Sunburst and Moondream and Snowglow.

I've barely got the last sign up when two guys from school come in. I sell them on the health idea and make them two super specials. They really dig them and keep bugging me about what's in them.

"Professional secret," I say.

As surely as people change heroes, they change habits, too. By eight o'clock that night, I'm selling health drinks as fast as I can make them. When I'm ready to leave, Freda has an unusual smile.

"You've tripled the fountain business," she says. "Quadrupled it. Jory, starting tomorrow, you get a raise."

The raise is only a few cents an hour, but in a week's

time it will add up. I'm anxious to tell Mom and Dad and I almost bounce through the door.

"Guess what?" Mother says. "Reve's coming home."

"Oh . . ."

"Aren't you glad?"

"Sure. I just—"

"What?"

"Nothin'."

"He'll be on the nine o'clock bus tomorrow night."

"Great."

"Jory . . . Did something happen at work?"

"Naw. Another day, another dollar . . ."

At the time I didn't realize that it was not abnormal to feel love and hatred toward the same person. And my feelings toward my brother were further complicated by something else of which I was barely aware. It was buried so deep that I even kept it from myself—as long as I could.

6

My feelings toward Reve may have been mixed, but when I see him grinning behind the bus window, I don't even try to be casual. And I've made up my mind: I'm going to tell him all that lousy stuff I once thought. I'm really going to.

Then he's stepping off the bus without an eyelash out of place. He's been riding for hours, and there's barely a crease in his uniform. Everybody's hugging and kissing and I offer my hand.

"Hi, Reve. Welcome home."

"Hey, Jory! How's it goin', man?"

"Great," I say.

And everything really *is* great. At home we have a big late dinner and everybody laughs a lot. I sit there thinking: How could I ever think that stuff about Reve? It all seems far away—the crazy ideas of a crazy kid.

In the living room, Dad and Reve are talking. I'm helping Mom with the dishes. Mom says:

"Your dad and I thought—maybe something wasn't right between you and Reve."

"Everything's fine."

"You sure?"

"Sure I'm sure."

And I was—then.

It's eleven when Mom and Dad go to bed, and I ask Reve:

"Want to see my zoo?"

"Your what?"

"Come on."

I take him out back and show him the graves. Then I'm telling him about Miss Elkins's car and the old dog we hit.

"Why'd you take the car, man? That's not like you."

"I don't know . . . It's—sometimes you just feel—crazy. Even the moon's—funny, sometimes."

Then I surprise myself: I'm actually telling him about the bird I killed. He kind of nods. There's the strangest expression on his face. Even in the moonlight I see it, and he's like someone I don't know.

". . . Crazy moon zoo," he says.

The mood and the time are right for me to tell Reve some things, but I don't. I try to pretend those unpleasant things are gone, vanished like those animals stuck in the ground by Reve's feet.

"Crazy moon zoo," he says.

7

When I'm not working, Reve and I spend all our time together. I don't even mind when he beats me at pool. At
the bowling alley, I notice people watching him. It's the
way he does everything with style.

The only difference in Reve that I notice is that everywhere we go he orders a beer. Even when we go to the
drive-in movie he takes a six-pack.

"You really like that stuff?" I say.

"It's OK. Somethin' to do."

That sounds like me, and it kind of bothers me that
Reve's twenty years old and he can still sound like me.

I tell him about Ellie, and he gets a kick out of me
having a girl. It's my idea for him to meet her and he
comes down to the drugstore the next evening.

Freda Norris almost does a Mexican hat dance when
she sees him. I make him a big super health drink and
we're sitting in a booth when Ellie comes in.

"You're Reve," she says. "I almost think I know you."

"In person," he says.

Ellie usually doesn't laugh a lot, but she gets to

laughing and I think maybe she's upset and is trying to hide it. She keeps tearing up straws, too—just shredding them in little pieces.

"You like the marines?" Ellie says.

"Yeah. Do you?"

She kind of blushes and says: "I like uniforms. You think I'd look good in a uniform?"

"Not exactly what I picture you in."

"I may join the service. I've been thinking about it."

"Why would you do that?" Reve says.

"To—get away. Just to get away from everything. Can you understand that?"

"Yeah."

And I'm thinking that's not like Ellie telling personal things to an absolute stranger.

"Oh, well," she says. "I probably couldn't get in anyway. I'm too fat."

"Don't say that," Reve tells her. "Think of yourself as curvaceous or—voluptuous."

"That last word," Ellie says. "Is that nice?"

Everybody laughs but I'm not at all convinced it's funny.

"Got a riddle for you," Reve tells Ellie.

"OK."

"What's black and white and red all over?"

"Come on, Reve," I say. "That's old as the hills."

"OK, wise guy. What's the answer?"

"A newspaper."

"Naw. A sunburned penguin."

Ellie laughs like it's the funniest thing she's ever heard, and I feel about three feet high. Ellie glances at her watch.

"I could stay forever, but I promised I'd be right back."

"I'll drive you home," Reve says.

"I can walk."

"Wouldn't think of it."

Before you can say the Gettysburg Address, they're heading out the door.

"Reve . . . Don't forget. I'm through at nine-thirty."
"I'll be here."

By closing time I've got the fountain polished mirror-bright. Freda's got most of the lights off.

"Where'd your dashing brother go?"

"Dashed out for a beer, I guess."

On the way home a lot of crazy stuff goes through my head; then I think maybe he had a flat. I'm walking with my hands in my pockets and I don't see this old guy until I almost bump into him. His breath all but knocks me over.

"Say," he says. "Don't I know you?"

"Aw, leave me alone."

I've gone about a half block and I turn around. That was the old guy—Dub—I was in jail with. I call him but he's lurching off up the street, almost out of sight.

I don't want to explain to Mom and Dad so I wait outside. It seems like a couple of hours pass before Reve drives up. He looks kind of sheepish, and I wait for him to speak.

"Man, I'm sorry. I really am. It's just that we got to talking and—"

"You said you'd be right back."

"I know."

". . . What'd you talk about?"

"You . . . Man, I'm sorry about the Science Prize. You should've won it."

"Win a few, lose a lot."

"Jory, you—you really like her?"

There was a moment when I could have told him the truth. But it wasn't my habit to level with people, so I gave him one of my famous shrugs.

"I—just—feel sorry for her, I guess. She *is* kind of fat and—she's poor and—everything."

"Beautiful eyes . . ."

"Yeah."

After I'm in bed I'm lying there getting all upset. That was stupid, not telling him how I felt about Ellie. It's like I betrayed her. I get up and walk down to Reve's room.

But I don't knock, I just stand there. I don't want him to know I'm hung up on a girl no one will date. I don't want him to know what I'm like—not Reve, of all people.

8

"Where's Reve?" I ask Mom.

She's in the living room with an atlas on her lap. She's always reading that old atlas, and she's got a pad and a pencil, too. It's almost one and I have to get to work.

"Out somewhere," she answers. "He didn't say where he was going."

In the last three days he's hardly been home an hour.

"He doesn't have much free time," I say. "He needs to move around a lot."

When Mom leaves the room, I pick up the atlas. There's a handful of travel folders stuck inside. On the pad is a list of cities: London, Paris, Rome, Athens . . . I join her in the kitchen.

"You plannin' a trip, Mom?"

"In my mind, Jory. Just in my mind."

"Why don't you take one?"

"We couldn't afford it," she says.

On the way downtown, I'm wondering why we can't afford it. It really doesn't make sense. I just always assumed we could afford anything we wanted.

The afternoon drags on and on. If it wasn't for the run on health drinks, I'd have nothing to do. Between concoctions I keep waiting for a call from Ellie. She usually phones in the afternoon. It's been at least two days.

When the store is empty, I call her house. I guess it's a younger brother who answers.

"Is Ellie there?"

"No. She gone."

"Is she out of town?"

"No . . . Boyfriend."

"*Boy*friend?"

"Ellie's got a boyfriend."

"What's he look like?"

"Big. Big soldier."

I work harder; I do everything twice. Polish the fountain and sweep the floor and dust the shelves which I dusted yesterday. I don't want to believe it: there's *got* to be another answer.

Just before I leave the drugstore I call home.

"Mom, is Reve there?"

"He came in and changed clothes. But he left again in the car."

"Did he say where he was going?"

"No. Said something about a date. Why?"

"Nothin' . . ."

"Oh, Jory," Mother says. "If the world was coming to an end, you'd shrug and say *nothin'* . . ."

There *are* other guys in the service, other soldiers, I tell myself. So I look in Pete's and I go by the bowling alley. Reve's not there and nobody's seen him.

He's not at Winslow's either, so I walk all the way out to the Good Buddy. When I see the car, I start running toward it. But there's not just one person in the front seat. They're sitting very close. One of them is Ellie.

For a long time I'm cool despite the heat. I trudge back

downtown and I go to the park. The lagoon's still there and the swans, but it's different. Even the trees sag in all the heat.

The moon is an eerie blue. It's not even a light, I think. It's a reflection. A weak, dumb reflection . . . like me.

My parents are in bed when I get home. I stretch out on my back, beneath a tree. The way I'm feeling, the sky could disappear and I wouldn't miss it. Who cares about dumb stars?

Come-ons, I think, like everything else. Dazzling, leading you on, then—the big rip-off.

I'm half asleep when Reve drives up. When he gets out to open the garage door, he doesn't see me.

"You're early," I say.

"What? Oh—Jory . . ."

He strolls toward me, nonchalant—King Reve—like nothing's happened.

"What're you doin' up so late?"

"Waitin' for you . . . Where you been?"

"Just—out."

". . . Why'd you do it, Reve?"

"What?"

"You know what. I called her house."

"Well—Jory, man I asked you . . ."

"Asked me what?"

"How you felt about her."

"You knew how I felt about her. You *knew*."

"You said you felt sorry for her. You said—"

"I know what I said."

"Then—what's the big deal?"

"The big deal is you. Reve Hall. King of the world."

"I don't get it."

"You get anything you want, don't you? Reve the athlete. Reve the outstanding. Reve the—"

"Wait. Hold on. You're really bitter, aren't you?"

"Should I celebrate? She was my girl, man. You sneaked around and—"

"It's more than that . . . Isn't it, Jory?"

"Aw, who gives a damn?"

I go around the house and I'm there in the backyard, leaning against a tree. For a while I don't know he's there.

"Jory . . . I guess—I should've known. I—didn't exactly think about it. We got to talking and—she's a real desperate little chick. She—"

"I know her. I know her pretty well."

"Do you? She's older than you, Jory. Not in years maybe but—"

"*Why*, Reve? Why'd you do it?"

". . . You want it straight?"

"Why not?"

". . . I've got—Jory, I don't have much sense when it comes to girls. I never did. You're different. You're much more level-headed than I'll ever be."

"That's great. That's really great. You knife your own brother in the back and then—"

"I told you the truth, man, and I'll tell you something else . . . It's no fun, Jory. It's like—it's sad, man. I didn't give *her* a second thought. Not as a person."

"Man, she's soft. She gets hurt easily. She's got lots of problems and you—"

". . . I won't see her anymore."

"You're noble, Reve. Really noble."

"Look, man, I'm kinda sick about it. Don't—"

"*You're* sick. How you think I feel?"

"I guess I know how you feel."

"No, you don't. Reve the winner! Reve the lady's man! Reve *everything!* How could you know how *I* feel?"

"Don't yell, Jory. They'll hear you."

"Why can't I yell? You do anything you want to. You always have. Why can't I *yell?*"

"Come on, man."

"Leave me alone. At least I can use my voice . . . Hey, moon! You're crazy! You're not even a light! You're a big *shadow!*"

The whole neighborhood can hear me and I'm waving my arms like a madman. Reve reaches out to touch me and I hit him. I connect solidly with his face and he doesn't even move. I've lost all control and I hit him again and he stands there with a trickle of blood on his mouth and he says:

"Jory . . . Man, don't . . ."

Mom and Dad come running out the door and there's no fight left in me, none at all. I go up to my room and it gets all quiet again. Then I come downstairs to get something to eat. Reve's out back, kneeling where the animals are buried. He doesn't move except to lift a can of beer up now and then like clockwork.

9

Concealing a quarrel in a family is like hiding a tree in a flower bed. Everyone was embarrassed. Each meal was an awkward, silent affair with each of us masking our discomfort.

Since Reve was at home most of the time, I simply stayed away until bedtime. Two days passed, and Reve announced that he was returning to base early.

Reve's upstairs packing, and I get the car out of the garage. I come in the back door and I tell Mom:

"I'm not going to the station."

"Jory—please do."

"No."

I've never seen her this upset and I don't like looking at her. I start out.

"Jory . . ."

"Yeah?"

"Don't let him leave like this."

"Like what?"

". . . I don't think you know him. You think he had

everything easy. Well, he didn't. And he feels things deeply, Jory."

"*Reve?*"

"You've always been the self-sufficient one. But Reve— we always had to reassure him, Jory. All through high school he—"

"He's grown now."

"Jory, he needs you. Needs what only you can give him."

"What's that?"

"Forgiveness . . ."

She waits for me to say something and I don't. I scuff into the living room. When Reve comes downstairs, our eyes meet for a minute. He's very solemn on the stairs, as though he's waiting for something important. I turn away and he goes quietly outside.

Dad's in the car with Reve and Mom stops on her way out.

"Jory . . . Don't let him leave this way. Tell him it's— all right. Just that."

"I—can't."

Her face kind of falls, as though something behind it melts. She leaves me with a sick feeling. I've disappointed her in a way I've never done before.

10

OK, *OK,* I tell myself in the mirror. You're not the world's worst *anything.* You're not the best anything, either, so what are you going to do—vanish? Practice laughing? Practice for life?

Tell you what, says Jory the Great. I've got this idea, see, about a chain of stores to sell health drinks. I'll start with—

No, you won't, Young Jory says. You'll work. You'll save your money. You'll—

Vegetate, says someone else.

I'm studying the mirror now. I'm so close I can see my breath on it. And I'm hearing this weird music—kind of a humming sound. There's something else there, too—in my eyes . . .

A shadow. Running . . . A man in the stadium? . . . No . . . It's me.

I'm dressed for work and I take a last look at the mirror. *Parents tell you all this stuff. They tell you everything but how.*

How can you laugh when nothing's funny?

There was an answer, of course—answers. For we *do* learn to laugh when nothing is funny. We learn to keep busy when there's nothing to do. We learn to like and even love when it is difficult to do so.

I'm not sure how others learn what they have to know. In my case, I didn't begin to learn these things until I *had* to . . .

11

I wasn't sure who was the worst—Reve or Ellie. But it was easier to blame it all on Reve. Certainly it was easier than facing those personal things, deep inside, with which I was uncomfortable. When I wasn't blaming Reve I was planning a national chain of small shops that sold Sunbursts, Moondreams, and Snowglows.

In my mind, I had built the idea into an international franchise the day that old Dubney Perkins came back into my life. When he entered the drugstore, I first thought he was all right. And then I saw his eyes.

"Well, well, well, well, well," he says. "My favorite jailbird."

I start apologizing for not recognizing him on the street that night.

"Say no more. No one apologizes to me. I apologize to the world. Sorry, North America. Beg pardon, South America. Excuse me, Europe. Forgive me, Af—"

"Dub, you're kind of loud."

"Oh. Thought that was someone else."

I talk him into a health drink and he sprawls in a back booth, nodding. Freda comes up and asks me if I know him.

"I've seen him around," I say.

A couple of older women waddle in and I make them ice-cream sundaes. Dub hasn't touched the drink I made. And when I'm serving the sundaes, he begins to sing.

"Car-ry me back to old Vir-gin-neeee . . ."

Freda gets to him first.

"You'll have to keep your voice down," she says.

"Right," Dub says. "Down voice, down. Down, boy. That's a good voice. Roll over, voice. Play dead."

"You're bothering my customers!"

"Then bring me something. I'm in great need."

"What do you want?" Freda says.

"A ham on rye and a stuffed goose."

"This *isn't* a restaurant."

"Then bring me the goose. I'll cook it myself."

"Dub," I say. "Come on, man."

"Come where?"

I don't know what to say, so I blurt something out.

"Come with me. I'll take you home."

That seems to please him, and Freda is very much relieved. We get to the door and Dub turns grandly around toward the two older women.

"Wrap up the old ladies," he yells. "I'll take them with me!"

"Dub," I say. "Come *on!*"

We're about halfway to his place and I'm struggling to hold him up. He lives in Southtown, and I'm thinking we're not far from Ellie's neighborhood. And I'm wondering what in the world I'm doing with an old derelict.

His house is older than mountains. Inside it's a swamp of dirty dishes, discarded clothes, and stacks of newspapers and paperback books. I get him into bed and he lies there like he's dead but his eyes are open.

"It's not funny, you know."

"What?" I say.

"Nothing. Nothing is funny."

"You were, this afternoon," I say.

"I *was?*"

For a few seconds the old guy actually reminds me of *me.* I'm not sure why I do it, but I find a little store and a pay phone. I call Freda and tell her I'm staying with him a while. Then I buy a jar of honey, some aspirin, a bottle of vitamins, and some room spray.

When I return, Dub is making Zs. I can't quite believe it but I actually clean up his house. There are only three rooms but it takes hours. I scrape layers of grease off the stove. I get colonies of mold out of the refrigerator. I open the windows and spray Floral Fiesta everywhere.

Then I gather up his old clothes. I give myself three merit badges for finding a Laundromat. Before I'm through I promote myself to Eagle Scout.

By dark the place is not bad at all. There's no electricity (I found some unpaid bills) but I discover three kerosene lamps. I get music on an old Philco radio and settle down with a paperback book.

"Where am I?" Dub says.

He's sitting on the edge of the bed, looking all around.

"Home," I say.

"Home," he says, like he doesn't believe it . . . "Home . . ."

Then he starts in about needing a drink, and I'm ready for him. I get the honey, the aspirin, and the vitamins.

"I read this article," I say. "Honey works wonders with drunks. Open your mouth."

He sits there like a kid and I feed him the stuff. I make him swallow three big vitamin tablets.

"Why are you doing this?" he says.

"Call me Jory Schweitzer."

He almost laughs. Almost. It's a thin, funny sound that gets to his lips and stops. But I can tell he's feeling better, and I offer to make him something to eat.

"I—I have to go out."

"OK. Fine," I say. "Go on and kill yourself. But first you can pay me for all the work I've done."

"Well, I sure—appreciate it . . . How much do—"

"For work like this at least four bucks an hour—for three and a half hours."

He nods and goes over to a bureau and takes something out. It's wrapped in tissue paper.

"I don't have much cash, but—you can have this."

It's a sterling silver necklace, tarnished, but it looks handmade. It might have come from another century.

"Aw, man, I don't want that. It's—personal."

"Could I pay you next week?"

"Aw, man . . ."

He puts the necklace back in the drawer and goes in the kitchen. I stand in the doorway.

"What're you doin'?" I say.

"Making coffee."

"Why?"

"Because—I don't have visitors very often. I want to—celebrate."

He doesn't look very celebratory. He's trying to get coffee in the percolator and his hands shake. He stares at them.

". . . Got a riddle for you," I say.

"All right."

"What's black and white and red all over?"

He thinks a minute and says: "A police car with ketchup on it."

That really cracks me up. I laugh so hard the old house shakes.

It's an odd life, but it's mine—no interference: no real Crazies messing it up, not even a shadow. I go to work; I save money; I go down to old Dub's.

At night we play pitch and hearts. We make huge bowls of popcorn. He tells me about the good old days when you could get a hamburger for a nickel and see a show for a dime. Alone with him I'm someone special.

It keeps me out of our house, and I don't see plans for trips nobody takes. I don't see medical books and I don't see Reve's room. I tell my parents I've got a new girlfriend and they seem pleased.

I have every reason to think the new arrangement will last. But it does not.

12

Dub's a different person. He's gone a month without a drink and he's not purple anymore.

"You're looking great, Dub," I tell him.

"Great? That's got to be an overstatement."

"How about good?"

"*Me*—good? Tell the truth, Jory. What I really look like is slightly warmed up."

Whatever it is, he's alive again. It's a Saturday and we're painting his house. We've been working on it for two weeks and it's almost finished. Dub turns and says:

"Got one for you."

"OK."

"What's black and white and red all over?"

I give up.

"An embarrassed mulatto."

I spill paint on myself and I laugh so hard I almost fall off the ladder.

Toward dark I go down to the little store—it's called a *bodega*—and I get us Cokes and stuff for sandwiches. It's a small store and I'm waiting to check out and there's Ellie.

"*Que pasa?*" she says.

". . . *Nada.*"

We just stare for a long time, and then I grab the bag of groceries and hurry out.

"Jory . . ."

I slow. I don't want to turn around.

"You forgot your Cokes."

When she hands them to me, our fingers touch.

"You—hate me, Jory?"

"No . . ."

"You've got a right to."

"That won't—help, will it?"

"Nothing will . . ."

I can't take looking at her. It's like she's twelve years old—and I'm ten.

"What are you doing down here?" she says.

"Helpin' this old guy paint his house."

"Mr. Perkins?"

"Yeah."

"No one in the world would do that but you."

"He's a lot better."

"You care for people, Jory. You really do."

"Well . . . look. I gotta go."

"Jory . . . If it's any consolation, I feel awful."

"It's OK, Ellie."

"It's not OK. Jory, I'm—pregnant."

The groceries are heavy as lead. Somewhere, someone is playing Spanish music: "*flores y amor,*" a voice sings . . . "*flores y amor . . .*"

"I haven't told anyone," she says. "I don't know what to do."

En todo el mundo
Hay nada
Nada pero flores y amor . . .

The only thing I can think of is that I can't let anything show. Nothing. I'm real cool.

"I'll send you Reve's address," I say.

And I walk away.

13

All the other times I've been able to pull out of it some way—at least keep moving. But nothing works. The city oozes heat and gas fumes, and I feel like I swallowed a slum.

Even the park is no help. Like sloppy marines, the trees stand in limp formations. And the lagoon is a swamp. I stare into its green, mossy depths, expecting The Blob to appear. Before I leave the park, I court-martial the trees.

Three weeks at attention! No water!

They sigh.

The entire, oozy city of Marshal sighs. Police cars creep past with their "sigh-rens" on. And out on the edge of town, somebody puts up a big, new sign: Have a Sigh-Burger . . .

So every day starts out like someone's birthday, and by evening it's Halloween with crazy pictures in my head. Dub takes notice of Jory the Droop.

"What's the matter?"

"Nothin' . . ."

"You know, you don't talk much about yourself. People need to talk. They need to share."

"Look. I've got to get back to work."

"I thought you were off tonight."

"I told Freda I'd—close up for her."

On the way to town, I think: How many lies does it take to make you a professional? Then I'm thinking: Why drag around all the time being *half*-crazy. Why not be a *real* Crazy and have some fun?

Freda's surprised to see me. I talk her into going home early and letting me close up.

When the front door is locked and most of the lights are off, I pace back and forth by the prescription room. The flashing head-pictures won't stop. It's like they're on the walls, too.

There's Reve up in his room, flexing his muscles . . . Ellie's eyes flicker like candles in front of a sad little grocery store . . .

And there's me: with a bunch of stupid animals in the backyard and one old bum for a friend.

I go in the prescription room. I know what I'm looking for. Other kids call it speed, but I know all the right names, the different brands. From each bottle I only take a few. I wrap them in blank prescription forms.

Behind the fountain I wash down a couple. I head for Pete's place.

14

I'm winning. And it's been a long time since I've won—
anything.

Two. Three. Four games, and I can't lose.

And I'm flying, too. The music's great and so am I:
Jory the Great. Who needs college anyway? I could make
it as a pool hustler if I had to. Better still, I'll get that chain
of stores going. I'll—

This dude I know from school comes in and heads
straight for me.

"Hey, man, what's wrong?"

"Nothin," I say. "Noth-*ing*."

"I mean that Spanish dude, Ellie's brother. He's really
lookin for you. He's been in here twice tonight. What
happened?"

"A mix-up," I say. "A crazy mix-up."

I get out of that place fast. I'm heading for the park;
then I think maybe he's there. Tall John. Glaring John.
I'm coming down, too, so I decide the best place to be is
home.

I'm about a half block away from the house, and I see
him: a tall shadow in our front yard, slouched against a

tree. I've heard those guys carry knives. I panic. I run back toward Main.

First I take another couple of hits. I'll go down to Dub's. But that's the *worst* place to be—the guy's own neighborhood. No, I'll stay inside Dub's house. I'll be safe. Dub will know what to do.

I come in the back door, and Dub is scrambling some eggs.

"Just in time," he says.

I plop at the table out of breath. He sets a plate in front of me.

"Not hungry," I say.

He sits and starts on the eggs. But all the time he's watching me.

". . . All right, Jory. What're you on?"

"Nothin'."

"Don't tell me that. I can tell by your eyes."

"So—big deal. I just took a couple."

"Of what?"

"Uppers."

"Speed?"

"Yeah."

"Where'd you get them?"

"At the drugstore. What are you anyway, a cop?"

"A friend."

"Friends don't hassle you."

". . . You have any more? . . . Do you?"

"A few."

"Let's see."

I shrug and take the pills out of my pocket and put them on the table. He unwraps them like they're alive. Then he grabs them and rushes into the bathroom. I hear the toilet flush. When he comes out, his hands are shaking.

"What'd you do that for?" I ask.

"So you won't end up like me."

"Don't worry."

"Jory—look at me. I've got nothing. No children, no wife, a shack for a house. Don't *do* that to yourself. *Don't do that!*"

Down the street some kids are playing. And someone's playing the phonograph.

En todo el mundo
Hay nada
Nada pero flores y amor . . .

"Dub . . . I don't know . . . I don't know what's going on."

"Drugs do that, Jory."

"It's not drugs. That was just tonight. It started long before that."

"Talk then. Talk. That's what happened to me. I held it in so long I—broke. *Talk.*"

"I don't *know* . . . You know me, Dub. Tell me something. Am I crazy?"

"No."

"Then—*why?* Why am I—"

I am about to lose control and I can't do that. Not Jory the Great. Dub scoots his chair up close.

"Jory . . . In the jail that night, you—you tried to be another person."

"I was scared."

"Maybe. But you didn't tell me the truth about anything. Not one thing."

"How do you know that?"

"I can tell . . . I've still got eyes, Jory. Senses. And I can read people—very well and very quickly—when I'm sober. You know what I saw that night?"

"Go on."

"I saw a boy who was running a mile a minute—from everything. From his friends, his parents, from girls—from himself."

"You only saw me for an hour."

"Well . . . You asked . . . And one more thing. I saw—a fugitive thing, fleeing, like a graceful animal, shying away under cover. A tenderness, Jory, that's what I saw. Some kind of inner fineness—a delicacy you were ashamed of."

Had I but had the courage, it might have been over. For he spoke of me, the real me, in a way no other person had. But until we learn better ways of behaving, we fall back on ancient reflexes. I was up on my feet, shouting.

"What are you trying to say? I'm not—delicate or anything. I'm as normal as anyone."

"I didn't mean—"

"Who cares what you meant? No one in town would listen to you but me. *Would they?*"

". . . No."

"OK, then. Save the lectures."

"It's because I care, Jory . . . You're like a grandson. You came here and—I got back my respect. Some of it."

"Then show *me* some, OK? You think it's a gas spending all your time with an old—"

"Say it."

"Aw . . ."

"Drunk?"

I go in the other room and stare at a paperback book. He kind of shuffles through the room. His hands are shaking. At the door he hesitates.

"What are you afraid of, Jory?"

"Who says I'm afraid of anything?"

"I do."

"Leave me alone, will you?"

". . . When I was your age, I had everything—health, ideas, a future. I was on my way to college, and it was something to go to college in those days. But—even then—there was this—*something* that separated me from other people. At first it was kind of like a haze, a fog. As I grew older it became thicker, darker. Finally—like a brick wall . . .

". . . I began to drink at first so that the haze would go away. I could see others better. They could see me. But the haze gradually turned into a wall. I realized a little late that liquor had done that. What I'd tried to escape with had built a prison around me . . ."

"I don't even drink, Dub. Why the sermon?"

"You've got some of those—signs, like I had. A certain kind of sensitivity—just below the surface. A fear of being hurt. A tendency to hide, even from yourself."

"Now you're my psychiatrist."

"Jory, it happens so *easily!*"

"Will you knock it off?"

"I couldn't—I couldn't bear it if something happened to you."

"Well, something's going to happen. I'm going to walk right out that door if you don't let up. OK?"

"OK . . . Would you like to play some cards?"

"No . . ."

Dub is standing at the front screen door. His hands are shaking. I should have heeded the danger signs, but I didn't.

"I'm going—out for a while," he says.

I say nothing.

And in my mind for a long time, I am running after him through moonlit streets filled with Latin music. I catch up to him and I take his arm.

Come on back, I say. Everything's fine. We'll have a big bowl of popcorn or something. Besides, I got one for you? What's black and white and red all over?

Who knows?

A salt-and-peppered fireplug.

Often in my mind is the sound of our laughing toward the small house and the glow of lamplight.

But that is not the way it happened.

15

For two days I put off going down to Dub's. I can't quite
face him yet. My conscience bothers me.

At home a kind of twilight seems to permeate everything. My mother walks through the house like a ghost.
Her face is tight, the color of milk. One evening when she's
out with some friends, I ask Dad:

"What's wrong with Mom?"

"I've been meaning to talk to you about that, Jory.
What do you say we go get a Coke?"

"Fine."

We drive down to Winslow's and for a long time
nothing is said. It is one of my favorite memories of my
father—his gentleness, his understanding.

I also remember the peacefulness of our being together. It was the last such peace I would know for some
time.

Dad says: "Mrs. Huerta called."

"Oh."

"Naturally, your mother's been quite upset . . . How
long have you known, Jory?"

"A few days."

"By the way, Mrs. Huerta said for you not to worry about John. She said John made a mistake. Does that—mean anything to you?"

"Yes."

"Did he think *you* were—responsible?"

"I think so."

"We called Reve tonight, just before you got home."

"What did he have to say?"

"He's pretty upset. He's coming home, Jory. He'll get an emergency leave . . . He said he wanted to do the right thing. What do you think the right thing is?"

"I don't know."

Dad doesn't look at me, but he says: "One of the differences between being a child and an adult is that you have to make decisions. You have to decide what's the right thing, whether you want to or not."

What my father said was not a put-down. It was both a clarification and an invitation. He was inviting me onto the stage where he was—a grown man.

"Dad, I . . . It's—the baby is the most important thing. Whatever is right has to be right for the baby. If I—if I was running things, children would come first."

I was proud of myself for that brief statement. It was the first time in my life I recall making a decision that did not put *me* first.

And when we were driving back, I kept thinking: *Nothing is what I thought it was. Not my parents or Reve or Ellie. Not myself . . .*

After all, I was just not that important. There were too many other people in the world—too many people with real problems. Like Dub . . .

Dub needed me and I had let him down. He was old; he was alone. To say the least, I had been unkind.

As soon as we got back home, I told Dad I had something I had to do.

16

But old habits do not die so easily. I was on my way to see Dub, but my mind was somewhere else—fighting.

First, it was the beer signs I saw along the way. They seemed to be everywhere. I kept wondering *why:* if that stuff got people in so much trouble, why was it advertised *everywhere*? Why did small children have to grow up looking at beer signs?

Or cigarette commercials plastered on billboards and in all the magazines. *Why?* In my city, the city on the moon, there wouldn't be any of that stuff . . . But then: Who was interested in *my* ideas, anyway?

The bookstore really did it.

It's a small bookstore on the edge of downtown. The store is closed, but the window is all lit up. And I'm standing there getting madder and madder outside the window.

Behind the glass are all these magazines. Girls with no clothes on. Girls staring at you, posing, winking, grinning, wiggling their fingers.

Why? Were children really the most important people in a society? If so, what was all this other stuff about? What were kids my age—and especially the younger ones—supposed to think?

Then I'm staring at a magazine cover, blinking my eyes. This naked guy is grinning. It's like Reve on that cover. *Reve.*

I pick up a rock. The glass shatters. An alarm goes off. I'm running down an alley, down another street and another block, and the alarm is still loud in my head. Dodging people, I make it another block, cross the street, and head into the park.

I'm there for a long time, getting my breath, watching the swans. I get to thinking I'd like to draw them. I'll get a sketch pad and sit there all afternoon. Who cares what a bunch of dumb guys might think?

"Who cares about anything?" I say aloud.

17

All day at work, I worry about Dub. I just can't get him off my mind. Reve will be home on the nine o'clock bus, but I can see him later.

I tell Freda it's important, and I get off a half hour early. I don't bother with supper. I run all the way to Dub's place.

"Dub," I call from the front yard. "Dub?"

The lamps are on and it's really quiet inside. Finally I go in and the place is a mess, almost like I found it before. In the kitchen I find empty beer and liquor bottles. I pick one up and break it in the sink.

I run back toward Main. I go from one bar to another. They're all like mausoleums with gray faces and gray music on the jukebox.

"Yeah, I seen him," this one guy says. "Staggered in here 'bout a half hour ago. Told him he'd had enough."

"Where'd he go?"

"How would I know?"

I'm running again, and up the street somewhere there's a siren, a flashing light. Something's happened on the street. I slow down. I don't like to see stuff like that. But I go on. They're putting someone into the ambulance.

A small crowd is gathered on the sidewalk. As I walk up, the ambulance is pulling away. I ask this guy:

"What happened?"

"They found some old man."

"Who was it?"

"I don't know. Some old guy."

"What was his *name?*"

"How would I know? Just an old drunk."

I start running after the ambulance, right down the street. People are laughing. Cars honk and tires screech. I can't catch the ambulance, so I cut across town toward the hospital.

Blocks and blocks and blocks run into each other—one long blur. I barely know where I am. My lungs are bursting when I get to the emergency room. The ambulance is parked just outside. I almost fall through the double doors. I ask this nurse:

"Where—is—he?"

"Who?"

"The old guy—you just—brought him in. I—gotta see him."

"I'm sorry," she says.

"I've *got* to."

"He was dead on arrival," she says.

I'm still fighting for breath. I can't believe I've heard her right. There has to be some mistake.

"Wait! Just—a minute. What was his name?"

"Perkins. D. Perkins."

Everything is white now, blurry, like the moon. I keep looking all around, shaking my head.

"You all right?" she asks me.

The lights are blinding. There's a sick blue smell everywhere. And for a time I don't know where I am. There are no landmarks, nothing to hold on to. Nothing. I have to *do* something.

"I want—I want to bury him," I say.

"I think you're overexcited," the nurse says. "You—"

"Write that down somewhere! Jory Hall, that's my name. You write it down. I'll be responsible. He doesn't have *anyone.* You hear?"

A big attendant starts toward me and I bust out through the doors.

And I can't run anymore. I just can't.

I'm covered with sweat. I'm hot; then I'm cold. The moon looks like a big hospital. I keep hearing things. Laughter. In my head I'm running out Dub's front door, and I catch up with him.

Got one for you, I say . . .

18

It's quiet in the backyard. Shadowy. The moon's so blue you can almost hear it. I move like a sleepwalker. I get a shovel out of the garage. I start digging out back by the alley. I'm talking to myself and the hole gets deeper and deeper.

The dirt is piled up three feet around me when the back light comes on.

"Jory?" Dad calls. "What—"

"I'm going to bury him," I say.

"Who?"

"It's OK. I'll be responsible. He needs—*some*one. I mean—there's no one . . ."

Dad's just staring and Mom comes beside him. And it's like the three of us are locked there. We're on hold.

Reve's there now, older in the hush of light. More real. Reve says something to them. They move away. They turn back. Reve ushers them toward the house.

In a half grave, I'm cold and I hurt. I hang on to the shovel like it's alive. Reve kneels in the dirt above me.

"What did you find this time?" he says. "Must be big . . ."

"A—a—man."

Reve has no definite idea what's going on, but he understands something my parents do not. He reaches down to where I'm standing, clutching the shovel.

"OK, now, it's just us, baby. Reve and Jory. You need some help?"

"I don't need anything! *Anybody!* You hear that? I can make it by myself!"

". . . I'll tell you something, man," he says. "I—can't. So for once in your life—help *me.*"

I don't believe that anything else he might have said would have worked. But that does. It takes a long time, but I let go of the shovel. I climb out of that hole and Reve is still kneeling. I stick out my hand and he takes it.

19

The lamp is a small sun in Reve's room. I don't know what time it is. I don't care. I've told him about Dub, and I'm still cool. I'm under control.

"You can't blame yourself," Reve says. "Dub . . . Things happen. Just like I can't go on blaming me . . ."

As the silence grows, I'm getting tighter and tighter. I tell myself it's all right to just let go and bawl or something. But I won't do that in front of Reve.

"You've got a helluva brother, Jory. You know that? . . . I didn't join the Corps because I loved it, man. I thought I had this chick in trouble. I ran . . ."

"Reve, I—"

"What?"

"I—one night—I . . ."

"Go ahead, man. Say it. It's just us."

I shrug and I say: "Nothin' . . ."

"Aw, man," Reve says. "You've been wantin' to tell me something for a long time. What is it?"

Still, I can't quite get it out. My hands on my knees are fists. My knuckles are white. And I remember Dub. I remember that face and all those years of being alone. I know I don't have much choice now.

"Reve . . . You were standing here by your mirror . . . I was in the hall . . ."

"Yeah?"

"I—hated you, Reve. I wanted to see you *hurt.*"

"Why?"

"I just—jealous, I guess."

"We get those funny ideas sometimes."

"But it's—the *reason* . . ."

"I don't get it."

"You—you'd just taken a shower. You were—you were the best-looking guy I ever saw. I thought you were—beautiful . . . And I thought—guys don't *think* that way and—I hated myself just for thinking that and—I started hating you, too . . ."

Almost immediately I am breathing easier. I can't believe I've actually told him. And I can't believe that nothing happened—no thunder; Reve didn't even frown. I've tortured myself for months and—nothing happened.

"Oh, man," Reve says. "We're so hung up about stuff like that. Even Dad. You know he can't hardly *touch* anybody?"

"Reve, I'm not—funny or anything. I'm OK. I just—"

"You're more than OK."

"No, I'm not. I've been a coward, scared of my own thoughts. I've been a liar and—"

"Jory, you cared for stuff that other people just left in the streets. You cared for a fat, sad girl that people joked about. And you cared for that old man. You—"

It seems as though Reve is going to lose control. That's almost as bad as when I do it.

"Reve, *don't* . . ."

"Man, you know what it is *not* to care—about much of *anything?*"

My brother is no longer a distant hero, winning trophies, or a shadowy threat to my masculinity. He's a twenty-year-old guy in a crumpled uniform with beer on his breath and tears in his eyes.

"Is there—anything I can do, Reve?"

"Yeah . . . You can be the best man."

20

The wedding is held in a small Catholic chapel not far from Ellie's parents' house. There aren't many people, only family, a few friends, and a bunch of loud kids. It's kind of like a movie—the kind you'd want to miss.

But Ellie is pretty in the blue dress she wore to the prom. And Reve looks great in his uniform. I get mixed up about which pocket I put the ring in, but after fumbling around I find it.

All through the ceremony I keep thinking about tall, glaring John. But he doesn't seem so tall after the wedding. He comes up and offers his hand.

"I make a mistake," he says.

"Me, too."

The reception is a thousand laughs with crepe-paper streamers hanging from the ceiling of the social hall and punch that tastes like Kool-Aid. As soon as Reve and Ellie leave, I cut out a side door.

I've decided what I have to do. I've caused enough trouble in one place.

21

I can't decide what to take with me, so I don't pack anything. I'll travel light. From my desk, I take the Moon City project.

In a couple of days I'll be in Houston, presenting my idea to NASA. I still may make the cover of *Time*. I might even end up rich.

Dad is just arriving as I walk out the front door.

"Where you headed, Jory? Can I give you a lift?"

"No, thanks. Just—for a walk."

It's looking like rain so I hurry on. I wonder how many lies I've told him in the past year. My calculator doesn't work that fast. But sooner or later they'll be proud of me. I'll write from Houston . . .

I don't know what made me go by the stadium. Saying goodbye to another boy-dream. Marathon runner Jory . . .

The gate is open. Coach has been holding early practice for football. I walk in and no one cheers. Jory the Great . . .

I sit on the bottom row of seats, the drawings beside

me. I wonder who that was up there watching me all those nights? Dub maybe. That's possible—but why? Or tall John. Maybe it was him.

A wind comes up suddenly and there's a cinder in my eye. The wind is damp and strong and I'm standing, trying to get my eye fixed, when it starts raining. When I turn around, my drawings are blowing all over the track and it's raining on them.

I try to pick them up and they're everywhere. It's like the last thing in the world I have, and it's getting ruined. I'm chasing pieces of paper like a madman. The ink's running on all the drawings, and I'm yelling:

"Don't! . . . Please, please *don't do that!* . . . DOOOOOOOOONNNN'T!"

Then I'm skidding across the cinders and I fall and I'm lying there in the rain, beating my fist against the ground. And way up high, someone yells:

"Jory? . . . *Jory!*"

He comes running down those stairs and then he's racing toward me across the track. As though he's God himself, he picks me up like I'm a kid. It's Dad.

"You hurt? Son, are you all right?"

"I'm . . ."

What I am is too tired to lie or run or make excuses. I can't even shrug.

"No," I say. "I'm not."

And then my dad is holding me against him and I'm crying as hard as the rain. I cry like I've just learned how and I don't care who knows it. He doesn't say anything. He doesn't have to. I can feel his strength.

When I can stop, I kind of pull away, and I say: "Why, Dad? Why all those nights, watching me?"

". . . I couldn't seem to get very close, Jory. I tried, but . . . I didn't think you wanted me around. So I'd just follow you over here. I loved watching you. It didn't matter what you did . . . Was I wrong?"

I nod my head no. That is just about the most beautiful crazy thing I ever heard of. It's like I've gone the distance.

He helps me pick up the wet drawings and we walk home and come in through the back door. Mother is at the table with the worn-out atlas. We're dripping on the tile and she hardly notices.

She says: "I suppose they'll have lots of brown babies. Brown, Catholic babies."

Dad doesn't know what to say, and I'm staring out back at some old graves . . .

22

Often in my mind is the sound of laughter, real or imagined. It is a precious thing in life: something, like God, I could not live without. The finest laughter I've ever heard is that of my nephew, who's now three. When I grow up, I want to be like him.

And I like to keep this last scene in my mind. It helps on winter nights when I study for exams until 3 A.M. It helps when I think of Reve and the job he doesn't like and how he lifts beer cans on weekends, one after another, like clockwork.

Mom and Dad and I are standing in the kitchen. It's just after Dad and I got back from the stadium. Mother has just made the remark about babies . . . I continue to stare at my private graveyard. But it's almost gone now—whatever it was I couldn't quite look at, couldn't quite outrun.

I face my parents. I know I can't take my mother on a world cruise. And I can't get my dad into med school. It's also quite possible that I may never make the cover of *Time*. For a moment, I feel helpless.

"Got a riddle for you," I say. "What's black and white and red all over?"

"A newspaper?" Dad says.

"That's old hat, Jim," Mother says. "It's a sunburned penguin." Dad laughs and I lean toward them: "Wrong again. It's an integrated beet."

The sound of our laughing swells through the house. Briefly, I was puzzled. But then I knew: *this* was the thing called life. And for the first time in seventeen years, I wasn't practicing.